Published by Semiotext(e)
PO BOX 629, South Pasadena, CA 91031
www.semiotexte.com

Cover photograph: Monica Nouwens
Design: Hedi El Kholti
ISBN: 978-1-63590-210-5

10 9 8 7 6 5 4 3 2 1

Printed and bound in the United States of America.
Distributed by the MIT Press, Cambridge, MA, and London, England.

PLAYBOY

Constance Debré

Translated by Holly James

Semiotext(e)

Part One

1

I didn't even dare use my tongue the first time I kissed a girl. That was after Laurent. I knew before but it was theoretical. I made an effort for the second one. I stuck my tongue right down her throat. She was a model, I felt flattered, like a guy. Things were going well. I was still scared, only less so. Except it never went any further than that. Or rather, they never went any further with me. Straight girls who were vaguely questioning their sexuality then giving up. Girls like me, only younger. With Agnès, it's different. She's fifty, she's married, she has children. She's a woman. I'm married and I have a son too but that's a different case entirely. Firstly, I was the one who left Laurent. And besides, it's just not the same. It's strange really, the fact I'm into her. I'm not even sure she's particularly attractive. I don't like her name. I never say it.

2

I show my card to security. I get a coffee from the machine. I smoke a cigarette. I put my lawyer's robe on. A friend tells me about the case he's working on. A court clerk says hi to me. Some tourists coming out of Sainte-Chapelle ask me Where are the toilets? I hope they enjoy the shit stains and the graffiti on the wall that says Arabs Suck Cock. I'm from the upper class, in case that much wasn't already clear. We even have a few duchesses on my mother's side of the family. That's why I speak like this. It's how aristocrats speak. They love it. I love it too. What you can't hear is the snobby accent. Which I also have, apparently. It might be because we're all bored shitless, the whole upper class, more bored than others that we speak like this. Just as bored as poor people. Really poor people. The ones from the projects and everywhere else. So we take it out on words. It lightens things up while we wait around for something to happen. I push open the padded door to the courtroom. The court usher's a good-looking guy. Not only is he a fag, he's also an Arab. Makes a change from the usual token hires. He lets me go first. I defend my client. Hash dealer, drug trafficking. If you can call that a dealer. If you can call that trafficking. I take my time pleading the case. I go up to the witness stand. The judges listen to me. I get even closer. It's not pleading. It's telling them what they want to hear. Good guy. Good school. Good family. The prosecutor is only calling for a suspended sentence. Judges go out on a limb for the middle class. That's how I met Agnès. I was defending her son. Of course he got off. Middle-class people never do time.

3

People don't call me madame, they call me maître. I do a man's job where you wear a robe. It even comes with this phallic necktie called a band that you can fiddle with in court. The robe doesn't usually look good on women. They're too short. Not me. Plus, black is a good color. The white band makes me look like an old Spanish aristocrat. I even get a sash with ermine along the hem. Actually, it's rabbit. But it still makes you look rich. The job suits me fine. No one sees my dirty jeans under the robe, no one wonders where I am if I'm not in the office, no one answers back when I'm pleading a case, no one monitors what I do, what I think, what I say. I like the guilty parties, the pedophiles, thieves, rapists, armed robbers, murderers. It's innocent people and victims I don't know how to defend. It's not the fact that they're guilty that fascinates me, it's seeing how low a man can stoop. Without even saying a word. Without even flinching. It takes a special kind of courage to get that low. It's not enough to have had a miserable childhood, alcoholic parents, or be poor with no prospects. Granted, it's a good start, but it's not enough. I like them, but I like them at arm's length. I'm not here to save them. If they get twenty years, that's not my problem. If they've had horrific childhoods and they end up dying in filthy prisons, that's not my problem. I'm just like everyone else, I'm here to get my pound of flesh. They have their lives, I have mine. I take a look and then I leave them in their squalor. I have my own. It's not as serious but it's no better. The important thing is to defend them well. And I do defend them well. It's not that hard. It's one of the few things I know how to do. That, and driving, I guess. There's nothing else, really. I don't think it's that big a deal. I don't think it's that important to know how to do things. Obviously it's not the best job. If anything it's mediocre. But at least I escaped office life, at least I don't have a boss, at least I earn decent money. I've always had a problem with money. Earning it stresses me out. It's only when I'm poor and the bailiffs are on my ass that I feel like I'm where I belong.

4

I liked her right away. I don't know why. Maybe it's the way she looks. The way she wears jeans. I just liked her. I didn't think too far into it. We were addressing each other formally. Then one day while she was on vacation, she started writing me, for no particular reason, with nothing particular to say. That's when I thought that she and I could have an actual love affair. Like with men. A real love affair with a beginning, middle, and end. And sex, obviously.

5

The essence of couple life is being bored shitless. Couple life and life in general. In that sense, we were compatible, Laurent and I. He smokes. That's his main occupation. The most essential relationship he has with the world. And why not? Before our son was born, the two of us were truly able to revel in our life of boredom together, wearing the same jeans, me taking his shirts. It was like that, that's the way it was with us. We were both the same height, we wore the same clothes, we were both as bored as each other. A solid foundation. Fifteen years of that. Neither here nor there. Calm. Like a bomb shelter. Fucking and love were additional extras. They were there, obviously, but they weren't the main attraction. There was a more fundamental understanding at the core of our relationship. Something that stopped us getting mad at times when we loved each other less. We didn't give a shit about that kind of thing. What we liked doing was waking up together every morning and saying How is it possible to be this fucking bored? We thought it was funny. It worked pretty well. It was when we became a three that it stopped working. Because of the food, I think. Going to the store on Saturdays to fill the fridge up with all that crap. All that time wasted preparing something that would only end up as shit. It was the food and it was everything else. The vacations, the stuff, all of it. There was no more space for emptiness. Laurent was happy. Everyone else was happy. I noticed the way people started talking to me all of a sudden. Trying to get me involved in all their sentimental bullshit. That idiotic joy of theirs. Everyone was delighted for me. Especially the people who'd known me since childhood. They all breathed a sigh of relief. They told themselves my little tomboy phase was over. Those are the kinds of things that made me leave.

6

She's ten years older than me. She has a career, an apartment in the fourteenth arrondissement, and a house in the countryside. She owns her place. She buys things on eBay. She takes the bus. She goes to the movies on Saturdays, brunch on Sundays, she likes Emmanuel Carrère, she never wears sneakers. Except in the summer, canvas ones. She drinks wine in the evening, either a white or a light red, local wines. Her cousins from the countryside send her recipes. She reads *Elle* and *Le Monde*. If there's a big protest, she'll go along. She votes left. She's highly disillusioned with politics but she thinks it's important to vote. She's never lived abroad, she doesn't really speak English. She's always worked for the same company. She thinks she's underpaid but she doesn't want people to know. She only has a few friends, friends who are richer than her, people she finds a little intimidating. But they're not real friends. She never goes out. Occasionally she has a work dinner, she drinks a little too much, she always comes home before midnight. Sometimes she feels a little sad and doesn't know what to do about it, so she waits it out. I decided that whatever happened between us would be the most important thing in my life. It didn't matter who she was.

7

I bought a second-hand scooter. I'm renting a one-bedroom apartment in the sixth. I've pretty much always lived in this area. In any case, I couldn't move too far from my son's school. Every other week, I pick him up on my scooter and drop him off at the gates. He hands me his helmet, bye sweetie bye Mom, I can't believe he's so tall, I can't believe he's him, I need to buy him new sneakers. Afterward I go to the café with some of the other parents. I listen to them all talking about the apartments they're buying. They don't seem happy. The guys are all bored and the women are worried about getting old. They all go to the same places on vacation. They end up in Megève, Biarritz, or Greece every summer. Maybe I'd be doing the same if I had money. Sometimes I feel like telling them they're all getting worked up over nothing. They'd be better off thinking about something else. They could easily survive without buying an apartment, without worrying about what tiles to put in their bathrooms, without leaving Paris for the summer. Vacations are such a pain in the ass. When I moved, I threw pretty much everything out. I kept two pairs of jeans, my jacket, a bed for my son, a sofa for me, and that's it. I left the cutlery, the crockery, the washing machine, and the furniture in my old apartment, the rest of my clothes and all the other crap went in the dumpster. I felt better right away. I go and buy a sandwich when I'm hungry. I like the Oliva from Cosi. Or the meal deal from the Japanese place that includes four skewers, cabbage salad, and a drink. They usually deliver within fifteen minutes.

8

Every Sunday we meet in the Jardin des Plantes. We walk a bit, we get coffee. That's how it started. Looking at the ostriches and the yaks, between her trip to the market and brunch.

The first sign of affection came from her. Without saying a word, she smiled and pulled me into a tight hug. A greeting, in silence, she held me in her arms for a long while. Her soft, matte, leather jacket. Her body, small against mine. That bistery brown smell of leather, musky, sweet, salty, earthy. Her perfume, and beneath the perfume, her smell, easily identifiable, detectable, distinct.

We'd have a coffee, then a second. A third even, later, when the weather started getting cold. We were stretching out time. I walked her part of the way home.

She put her hands in her pockets. As we walked, I took her by the arm, just above the elbow. That feeling again, her slender frame beneath the coat. A woman's bones feel so delicate when you're used to men.

The moment comes when it's time to say goodbye to her, when I hold her, when I breathe in her scent. I don't know if it's desire. I don't know what it would be like to kiss her.

At some point she suggests addressing each other informally. I'm the one who finally dares to do it, months later.

She says she'll go for dinner with me. She asks me if I'm in love. She tells me she's met someone. I don't know if she's talking about me. When she talks about love, it's always about men. She tells me she took a shower before coming.

Sometimes I get annoyed at myself for not being brave enough to do anything. Once or twice I let on that I'm angry or frustrated. She doesn't say anything, she doesn't seem to take offense.

She comes to my place for the first time. She smiles, she barely speaks, she looks at me. She says I'm beautiful, she asks where my bed is, I don't move. She gets up, she puts her coat back on, I get up too, she slowly fastens the belt, she doesn't leave, she looks at me, she seems to be waiting for me to do something, I'm too scared. That's exactly what I tell her, I'm too scared.

Beneath my thumb, when I go to say goodbye to her, the curve of her breast under the felt of her coat. So light and fast that I'm not even sure. I close my eyes, yes, it was her breast.

9

I never really understood why people think having junkie parents is such a bad thing. My sister and I still managed to have a blast. Especially after my mother died. We had some great times with our dad, the shrinks, the fire brigade, and all the rest of it. Like the time we forgot which day we were supposed to be handing the apartment back, and we turned up in the street with the trash bags, the vacuum cleaner, and the Mr. Muscle Fresh Pine in the back of the car, and the English owners were already standing at the window, they took up smoking again there and then when they saw the state of the studio apartment, and Dad just sat there on the couch, not saying anything, drunk. My mother was a different story. My mother was spectacular. Everyone would stop and look at her. Young people, old people, dogs, children, rich or poor, ugly or beautiful. She could ask for anything. She always got it. If ever the police stopped us in the car, she just had to say one word and they would let us go, their cheeks turning red. It was crazy. My childhood memories are of me looking at her. Me and my father looking at her. It's different for my sister. She doesn't really remember. She was too young when my mother died. And those were the dark years when they didn't have enough money for heroin. They started drinking. That, my sister remembers. Heroin wasn't as nasty. All it did was send them to sleep, cigarette in hand, and occasionally the bedsheets would end up in flames. The meds came after that. My father's true specialty. But the best was the opium. The pipes, the lamp, the smell. That was when I was really young. It was like Saigon. My sister and I were talking about it the other day. She thinks they were completely insane. I think it's normal lives that don't make sense.

10

When school's out for winter break, she invites me to the countryside for the first week of vacation. It's her grandfather's farm, she bought it from her sisters. She tells me he used to wash himself once a week with a washcloth in the kitchen. She shows me a photo of him. A farmer with very dark skin and a very wrinkly face. It looks like a postcard. She's the successful one in the family. Her parents were teachers. It was a big thing for them, Mitterrand getting elected, his march to the Pantheon and all that. She's converted the old stable into a living room and decorated it in light colors. There are paperbacks of Flaubert, Balzac, and Dostoevsky in one corner of the room.

Her husband isn't here. She never talks about him. In the beginning I thought they'd split up. But maybe that's not the case. Because they definitely still live together. The first time she mentions him, it's to tell me he refers to me as She Who Must Not Be Named. Like Voldemort in *Harry Potter*.

I guess she's brought me here because she wants something to happen. One night when I get up to go to bed, she takes me in her arms and holds me, for ages, without saying a thing. I want to pull away, I go to say something. She holds me tighter, she tells me not to speak. She does it again twice over the course of the week, the beginning of something, a gesture. Later she referred to those moments as embraces that speak for us.

I think she has a lover she sometimes calls. I tell myself she doesn't want me because she has a lover. I tell myself you can't love two people at the same time. I ask myself what the hell I'm doing there, why she asked me to come, what the point of it all is.

11

I wasn't used to being in love. It reminded me of when Laurent cheated on me with the intern. I told myself it was interesting to live through something so banal, that it was exactly the kind of experience you should have. The most important thing was to hold on. To really want it. The whole thing had a touch of *Werther* to it. It was fascinating.

12

I remember Uhart. I remember my mother and aunts sun-bathing on the rooftops, diving into the Nive river, icy cold, the mornings when I'd go to see the horses while it was still cool out and everyone was asleep, I remember the church, the men upstairs, the women downstairs, the Basque hymns. I remember the old horse my mother had, a mare called Pika. I remember the dinners the grown-ups had, their conversations, their arguments. I remember being in the maid's quarters one summer, after the fire, I remember the storm. Those are all things that don't exist anymore, the château was demolished, they sold the grounds. I found a photo of my christening, that was there too. My mother is wearing a light, short suit and white boots, she's holding me in her arms. I'm wearing a long, old-fashioned dress made of lace. My grandfather the prime minister is there, the shortest of the group. And my father, young and thin, in a brown suit and a green Arnys tie I later found in Touraine.

13

Now it's my turn. I invite her to go away. It's a place in the Basque country but this time by the sea. It's a place in the Basque country but it's not mine. I'm crashing at someone's house. During the day I go surfing, she reads on the beach. She didn't want to try, she must think she's too old. I get out of the water. I unzip my wetsuit. I see her casually turning her head to look at my breasts. In the evening I take her for drinks at a tapas bar by the sea. It's still daytime, she makes comments about guys' bodies as they walk past, All surfers are hot she says. I'm wearing battered red espadrilles and an old pair of jeans. That's how rich people dress. She's wearing shoes she thinks are chic and a spotless pair of pants. I'm always a bit embarrassed by her when we're around other people. I'm drinking ginger mojitos. She's drinking wine. I don't like it when she's drunk. She's hungry, she wants to try the local specialties. She thinks everything's incredible, my espadrilles, my ginger mojitos. I always feel a bit like I'm a character with her.

In the evening, when I say goodnight to her in the doorway to her room, she looks at me differently. I don't say anything, I don't do anything, I wait to see if she has the guts. I go to bed. From her bedroom, right next to mine, she texts me saying Every time I tell myself next time.

14

The fact remains that people don't really think. I can almost understand it with poor people. Though the more I see them, the ones in prison at least, the more I think they're thinking pretty damn hard. But everyone else, the vast majority of people living more or less cushy lives, it never seems to cross their minds that one day, they're not going to wake up. I can't comprehend their lives. I tried to be like them before but it didn't work out.

I gave everyone the shock of their lives when I was four. My great-grandfather the medical professor they named the hospital after insisted on me having brain scans. The man of progress himself thought the fear of nothingness might show up on an MRI. Obviously they didn't find anything. So they sent me to a shrink for kids. I took her dolls and pretended to make them piss on her carpet. She didn't bat an eyelid. She may have wanted to smack me but she didn't bat an eyelid. I went back to school. They decided I should skip a grade. I gave up with the worrying. You get tired of everything eventually. Everything, my dear. I dealt with it. Or I moved on to something else.

People get scared by the slightest thing. I get bored by the slightest thing. That's the difference between them and me. And I can't believe my luck.

15

It's almost summer. She's gone to the South for work. She sends me pictures of her Airbnb. She says she'd love to live in that kind of apartment. The whitewash seems to have made an impression on her. She texts to ask if I want to join her. Tomorrow. I jump on the first TGV. In the afternoon, we walk around, we go sightseeing, we always have to say how nice everything is. In the evening, she talks about Sagan and Colette. She went to prep school. I go to bed.

I don't sleep well. When the sun comes up I take off the men's shirt I sleep in, I tie it around my eyes to block out the morning light. She comes to wake me up, she sits on my bed, she places her hand on my hair, then on my bare back. It's the first time she's touched me. I don't move, I don't speak, I am my back, I am her hand.

I see her breasts for the first time. The first rays of sun, the icy-cold Mediterranean Sea. We don't have swimsuits.

She undresses. The violence of her skin, winter white, the fabric of her lingerie, slightly loose, the violence of her breasts, still beautiful. She takes off her bra, keeps on her panties, the violence of another person's body. I close my eyes to what I don't want to see. I follow suit, I take off my T-shirt to swim. I keep on my shorts, cut from an old pair of jeans. We lie down, she falls asleep, I close my eyes. We get up, me behind her, my arm around her neck, my chin on her shoulder.

It's the move that will never be made, the thing that keeps slipping away, the thing we've gotten used to not doing now, getting closer and closer yet more and more abstract. For months it's been like this, these advances, infinitesimal and slow. It's so slow. I've never known anything to be so slow. I'm almost used to it by now. I don't know what it takes to spark desire.

16

It would have been easier with a man. We would have kissed, we would have slept together, we would have tried. Either way we would have known what to expect. There wouldn't have been all these months of smiling at each other and not feeling brave enough to do anything. It's easier with them. We send out signals and leave it to them to make a move. We leave the question of courage to them. I don't know when I realized it would be up to me. The thought scared me. I liked it, too. I liked the idea of being the boy.

17

I leave my phone in the car. I show my card, my license, they give me an old copper token and a badge that says authority of the law. I take off my belt, I hold my jeans to keep them up, I always have this problem with pants, I empty my pockets, I go through the scanner, I put my things back on. I cross the courtyard. Dirty and gray. I get my token out. I go through the metal gates. Fresnes Prison, division 2. Lawyers' room. I wait for him there, the smell of the canteen wafts in. Sentence-adjustment hearing. He says If I get out, I'll only do one more. He says It's not about the money, it's about the adrenaline. I tell the judge he's gone straight, I talk about the charity, I show the paperwork. Distributing books to the poor, that's his project. The judge looks at him. I think to myself He's too beefy, the least he could have done is go easy on the pushups. The face is a lost cause. But the judge doesn't seem to notice. Besides, he's fifty-eight. You don't do holdups at fifty-eight. That would just be reckless. Maybe she does notice but she doesn't give a shit. She lets him go. On day parole to begin with. He can distribute his books during the day, but he has to spend every evening in some ridiculous center in the middle of nowhere. They're not going to give him his life back just like that. That's the procedure, he's used to it. His tattoos tell his life story. A broken chain, the names of his children, women he's loved. Old-school designs for an old hand. He's spent half his life in prison. He's never made much money. Just enough to bum around for a while in the shitty projects he lives in, waiting to go back inside. He says he has no regrets, it's been an adventure, that's just his life. He shakes my hand. He thanks me. There really is no need. I take my card and give the token back. I can't even go to the bathroom to wash my hands, there's never any soap.

18

I tried imagining the sex. I tried to get myself off thinking about her. It didn't work. Nor did the lesbian category on YouPorn. Not really. I said to myself it didn't mean anything. I said to myself Let's just see.

It was going to take more radical action. Radical but easy. I didn't want to overdo it. There are only so many things you can do that are both radical and easy. I asked her to come to Italy with me. She said yes. I thought it was quite a big deal, agreeing to go to Italy with someone who has a thing for you. But I knew I couldn't be sure of anything with her. If nothing else it'd be a trip to look back on.

I bought the tickets, booked the hotel. It wasn't really a hotel, it was a big apartment in an old palace. In the photos it had huge rooms, books, paintings, piles of stuff, carpets, sofas, colors, all chaos and affluence. It belongs to a French guy who lives there over winter. I recognize his name. He recognizes mine. That's exactly the kind of thing I can't tell her. She'd think it was a big deal but it's not.

We missed the plane. She insisted I buy new tickets. I bought them at the airport on my phone. I was annoyed because I didn't have any money. She knew I didn't have any money, she pretended she'd forgotten. I don't know when it was established that I would always be the one picking up the check. In a way, it suits me. I don't want to owe her anything. The payment was accepted. We had to change airport, make a stopover in Germany. Then finally, the heat, the evening, the roofs. It's a beautiful location, it's Rome, it's summer. There's that at least.

The languid hours, the afternoon, a terrace, the rooms, a fan. She goes to take a nap. She texts me and tells me to join her. She adds a smile emoji. I can't even begin to describe how much I hate emojis. Obviously I go. She's lying on her bed. She's wearing panties and a T-shirt. It's the upper thighs that show the first signs of age in women. I lie down next to her. I stroke her shoulder, I move closer, I push her hair aside and press my lips to her neck. She doesn't move, she doesn't say a word. I stop. Maybe she's sleeping, maybe she's just pretending to. I can't see her face, she doesn't move. I'm lying on my stomach, my head to one side on the pillow, I don't dare to do anything, I wait for ages, my neck hurts. Ambiguity is cowardice. I hoist myself up onto my elbows, I lean over her, I kiss her. Now

I know it's possible. Things are starting to happen. It's the beginning of something.

After kissing we go out for a walk. I think she wanted us to sleep together there and then. I wasn't thinking about that. I wanted to walk around Rome with her. She doesn't mention what happened as we're walking through the streets, she doesn't say anything about how long it took, she doesn't mention love. Her smiles haven't changed. She doesn't make a single gesture different from the ones she made before.

We have dinner, we go to bed, she doesn't say anything, she doesn't do anything. I sleep outside on the terrace. At some point I feel someone putting a sheet over me. She never mentions it afterward.

The next day. We walk, it's hot, she wants to go sightseeing, I'm getting a little bored. We go for dinner. The food's bad but she says it's good. She has a few drinks. We go back. The palace, nighttime, the heat, the enormous rooms. She's forgotten her glasses, I go back to the restaurant to get them. The city, the staircases, everything's beautiful tonight. When I get back she's out on the terrace. We chat, it's late, I'm lying next to her on some kind of sofa or bed, where I slept the night before. I don't know how it all happens. Suddenly I stop thinking. Suddenly I want her and I lean in toward her. I kiss her, I slide my hand beneath her T-shirt, I stroke her breasts, I kiss them. Breasts and love. Of course. I understand something I didn't know before. It all just happens. I unbutton her pants. Desire makes everything so easy, there's no awkwardness, nothing strange about the movements I'm making. I take her to her room. I smile when I unclip her bra. I don't know which one of us takes off my clothes. I stroke her body. I'm the one on top of her. I'm the one kissing her breasts, touching her cunt. I'm the one who fucks her. Her eyes roll back and her face is taut when she comes. She falls asleep.

At five in the morning, the light is still gray. She's the first thing I see when I wake up. A naked woman lying close to me. She's on her side. Sleeping. Her back, her shoulders, her ass. I see all her beauty, the beauty of women, I see my own body, new. I tell myself There are lots of things that are possible.

In the taxi, she says You knew. Knew what? When we get back, she acts like nothing happened. More or less.

19

They're practically giving stuff away here, that's one thing at least. My favorite thing to do is go to Super U. I go twice a day. There's nothing else to do anyway. I look at the special offers on processed food for big families, poor families, and families who don't care too much. I try on the clothes, they have some very wearable sweaters, shame they're acrylic. I leave with a can of tuna, bread, coffee, tomatoes. Even my shopping cart says I'm not from here and I'm not like them. I can tell from the cashier's face. I keep my sunglasses on to divert her attention from my ripped APC pants and my snobby accent that slips out when I say No, I don't have a store card. My father doesn't talk. Neither do I. Sometimes we force ourselves to pretend to be a normal family. He asks about work. I reply. I don't tell him that I do jack shit. I don't tell him that I don't care anymore. That it makes me sick. That I'd rather swim and read and think about what's happening in my life. I don't tell him what's happening in my life. I tell him that things have never been better since I left Laurent. I tell him that Italy's beautiful. I take my son to the local swimming pool, next to a campsite. We go fishing. The Loire is beautiful. There's a smell of silt in the air but it's still beautiful. We read comics in the garden. None of us knows whether we're relaxing or bored shitless. In the train home I ask him How did you think Grandpa seemed? He says Not too bad. He says He's drinking less. I say It might be because they upped the Subutex. There was no ticket inspector in the train. We get Japanese food to celebrate. Soy milks all around.

20

She has a lover. Several, maybe. The day after our trip to Rome, she tells me she's spending the coming weekend with an old lover. She's also seeing another man during the week, a very good friend of hers. She says But I'm cheating on all of them with you.

She never talks about love, she never mentions what happened in Rome, what's still happening in Paris, I have no idea what's happening, either.

I go to her place, she's working. I go to kiss her when I arrive, she says No, not like a lover.

Sometimes she comes to my place. We sleep together. She comes fast. She says That feels good, it feels so good. She never stays long and when she leaves she says I should never have come, I knew that would end up happening.

She's alone. She invites me over. She says she shouldn't, she has work to do. Wine, cheese, dinner. Every time I see her, something has to be broken, I have to find my way back to her. I get close, I coax her, I lean in, I kiss her. Every time I have to pluck up the courage again because the things that have already happened don't entitle you to anything. She says I'm not going to drag you to the bed. She tells me to wait for her there. She goes into the bathroom. I have no idea what women do in bathrooms. There are family photos on the bedside table. I wonder whether she does this often. I make her come, she lets me go down on her this time. Lying next to her, I tell her about Rome, about waking up and seeing her beauty that first night, that first time, while she was still sleeping, I tell her it was a beautiful moment, the gray day over the rooftops at five in the morning. She starts shaking her head, she says she doesn't want to hear it, she says No, you have to be kidding me. We smoke a cigarette at the window, she doesn't ask me to stay over, I leave.

The pleasure of being the one who leans in. When I'm lying down, and I get up onto my elbows, when I lower my body or tilt my face, when my body supports me, when I'm kissing her, her body in my hands, when I'm holding her by the hips, the shoulders, the nape of the neck, when I'm kissing her and it's my hands stroking her body, or touching her lips, ever so lightly, when it's my mouth, or when it's my hand, firmly grasping her ribs. A body at arm's length, a body held close, a body held tight.

One night she comes over to my place. She tries to touch me. She's clumsy. She gets upset, as if I'm a man and I can't get it up. There's never any tenderness.

I can count all the times over this summer on one hand. Four. I don't know what I'm keeping tally for. I swim six times a week.

21

You have to get there before eight to be able to swim before the school kids arrive. On the weekends, I go a little later. I bought a black Arena swimsuit from Au Vieux Campeur. It's plain, it makes you look like you mean business. And little Swedish goggles. They're not from Sweden but that's what they're called. I take my shower there now. Everyone does in the morning. The regulars. We've started getting to know each other. There are men's showers and women's showers. It creates a certain atmosphere. Most of the women do what I do. We pull our swimsuits down to our asses. There are some who take theirs off completely but I feel weird about standing there stark naked. At first I didn't really like seeing their bodies. Now I'm used to it. We wash and we talk, or we don't talk. It depends on the day.

I got the idea from Emmanuel. It was one of the first things he told me about himself, that he goes to Pontoise swimming pool every morning. It's simple, it's serious, I was impressed. He's tall, slim, always chic, and he's also a fag, so that's why I wanted to do it too. I told myself I would be a different person if I were capable of doing that. I started when I got back from Rome. Before that I used to fence. But I wanted something new. A new form of discipline. Something transformative. The scooter, boulevard Saint-Germain, the cubicles with their blue doors overlooking the pool, the swimsuit, the water, the laps. One hand plunging in, accelerating underwater alongside the body, the other relaxed, effortless, the elbow above, driving it back, legs drawn out behind for support, eyes looking down into the blue interior of things. I swim, I'm weightless, the water, the silence, the pleasure of dexterity, the simplicity of exercise, the use of the self.

22

I ran into Robert in the street. We got coffee. He says
Heroin is an eraser, heroin erases everything. He's a
friend of my father's from twenty years ago. There was
him, Henry, and a few others. They had their little
group, smart guys, smart as only they could be, doing
drugs because when you think about it what else is there
to do apart from getting yourself in trouble and falling in
love and the whole thing blowing up in your face every
time. I run into him a lot since moving. He lives in this
neighborhood too. When he sees me, he throws up his
hands, he shouts my name, he asks if I have five minutes.
He always smells good and I always have five minutes.
Five minutes with Robert ends up being more like an
hour. He tells me his stories and I listen. They used to
spend more or less every day together back then. They
went to each other's houses. I liked them. I don't know
when they ever worked. But they didn't work much.
Sometimes their kids would be there, getting under their

feet. When it came to women, they did what they could. Robert talks about the white stuff, the good stuff from Marseille, the stuff you could still get twenty years ago, practically pure. He says Heroin's almost gray now because they cut it with so much other stuff, he points at a newspaper, *Libération*, to show me the color he means. Coke in the right pocket, heroin in the left, twenty years they went on like that. He's more or less clean now, except for a gram of methadone every day and the occasional line. It's a miracle they didn't die, all three of them. As a child, he tells me, he was so scared of everything he had the shits constantly, his nanny used to send him off to school with a pack of Imodium in his pocket. He says he found a photo album behind the radiator on boulevard Haussmann. The cover was a garnet-colored velvet. Inside there were pictures of corpses, corpses from the camps. It seems to mean something to him, the fact that he's Jewish. The same goes for the drugs, for everything. He says when he sells the gallery he'll pick up his car in Monte Carlo and head for Russia via Odessa. And it's all because of Léna. A girl he loves who doesn't love him back.

23

A woman is a very strange thing. Radically different from anything else. I don't know when I started thinking that. Maybe when I looked at her lying there next to me that first morning, when she was sleeping and I wasn't. I started comparing our bodies, our breasts. I knew before that I had no hips, that my breasts were small, that I was taller and thinner than most other women, but it was just a vague notion. I stood in front of the mirror at the swimming pool to try and understand. Maybe the crawl had accentuated the outline of the shoulders and canceled out the hips. My body is me, no more, no less. It's been right in front of me all this time. I started comparing myself to her. I saw myself and I saw her, her and all the other women I'm not. The shoulders, the suppleness, the roundedness, all the things she has and they have and I don't. I measured her up and I measured myself up too. Physically, morally. I thought, A woman is something I had never imagined. Something more bare and more raw than a man. Something perpetually verging on obscene. That's what she made me realize. Men don't get under your skin. Maybe they don't have the same capacity to move you, either. But they don't get under your skin. Yes, maybe it started the first time I saw her naked. Maybe it was later. When I saw that she didn't want to give me anything. When I felt her dry hands on my body. When I saw her with her children, slowly devouring them, her mind at rest, her heart at peace. When I realized that she prefers things to people, not even the big things, but the small things, the most insignificant things. When I understood there was nothing she desired from the world. That's when I thought, So that's what a woman is, soft skin and stupidity, a narrow soul that can't compare with the softness of the skin, sloppy caresses, a body that can't return the reverence it inspires, an animal that knows nothing of love and desire, that knows nothing of beauty either, a bourgeois body, devoid of greatness, slightly dirty. It's someone who cries when they're being mean. To love a woman, is to despise her. I understood the violence of men. I wondered if that's how they had always felt about us, if that's how Laurent had always felt about me.

24

It's not like she was any worse than the others. Perhaps a little weaker, a little more ridiculous. We were in seventh grade. It became a craze. Everyone started doing it. In the boys' bathrooms, then the girls', then outside the bathrooms, on the tables, the blackboards, the walls, everywhere, in ballpoint, felt-tip pen, Tipp-Ex, etched with a pocket knife: Lejeune is a whore. Even the kids she didn't teach got involved. Even the teachers' pets, even the kids who never wrote anything on the tables, even the shy kids, the ass-lickers, the pussies. It was a silent, spontaneous movement, no program, no leader, a movement consisting solely of this graffiti, and we all thought it was wild. A movement of joy and rage that stirred up a high school where nothing ever happened. The beauty was in the gratuitousness, the absurdity. It had nothing to do with the teacher, no one gave a shit about her. When she cried we all felt ashamed. Not of our ourselves. Of her. We wanted to be caught in the act, we wanted her to yell, we wanted her to get even, to give us bad grades. We wanted her to tell us she wasn't a whore instead of crying. She left after fall break, we never saw her again, we found other games to play.

25

Paris, fall. She comes to meet me in cafés. She comes to see me often. She writes me every day. When I invite her to my place she says I can't. Sometimes she kisses me or lets me kiss her. She doesn't say anything, we never talk about it. She says she's going to leave her husband. I don't know if that has anything to do with what happened between us. Or what's happening between us. I don't even know what's happening.

She says they made the decision this summer. She says they're no longer in love. They've always been very free. Free, she says. They don't sleep together anymore. They each have their own lives. She can't understand why he hates her sometimes. They haven't spoken about it to anyone. She doesn't dare. It's shame that keeps her there. She says divorce is failure.

We meet in a café. She brings me a piece of cheese, big enough to fill an entire cheeseboard, greasy, yellow, sweating, stinking, stupid.

Speaking in hushed voices, the presence of her body, right there, her every breath. Other people. In the doorway, hidden away, a look, a kiss.

Her walk, the slight sway, her back, straight as an arrow, the slight arch, the long thighs, skin that's tanned and smoothed by the sun. It's almost chilly out. White T-shirt under a navy-blue sweater, her mascara, her perfume.

She slides her pelvis toward the edge of the low armchair and spreads her legs slightly, in the shape of a *V*, legs bent, shoes beneath her knees, torso straight. I know the weight of her head in my hand, her hot palms, I know how she smells too, I know it all with my eyes closed.

She comes over to my place. She tells me her husband asked her if she's leaving him for me. I don't know why she's telling me this. She won't leave him. Kisses on my bed, fully dressed, I lean in toward her breasts, she pulls down her sweater and shakes her bangs into place. She says she doesn't have time, she looks at herself in the mirror, she smiles, she says We're beautiful, she's looking at herself.

I go downstairs. She's waiting at my door. I'm on the phone, I have my arm around her neck, the smell of her. Tepid tea, the gray light of the day, why am I putting sugar in this tea. She says Don't look at me like that. She smiles.

She wants us to go to the gym together, I think it's to put the secret out there in the world, I think it's to see how much I'll say yes to. Maybe it's just because the subscription will be cheaper if I go with her. I say yes.

She asks to see the notebook she gave me, she stuck photos inside, tickets, a map, and a few ambiguous sentences. I'm sitting in front of her, the sun is streaming in through the windows, we're alone, she's in an armchair in front of me, she doesn't look at me, she doesn't touch me, she looks at the notebook, she smiles.

I look at her, I hesitate, she says yes, I kiss her. It's funny how it's always up to me to kiss her. She's the one who decides when.

The things I don't understand don't exist. I suspend all curiosity regarding her absence, her ways, her reasoning. All that happens is all that exists.

She tells me to expect a letter. It's a photo of me taken by her that comes in the mail. One sentence that could mean everything or nothing, typed up on a computer, no date, no signature.

Having lunch, in the sun. Out of nowhere, she grabs my arm, takes my face in her hands. Her hand around the back of my neck when we leave.

Every day she writes me, every day I see her, her smile never changes, her texts are all the same. I don't ask any questions. She keeps me there at arm's length, slightly more than a hypothesis, slightly less than reality.

She says she's looking for an apartment. She doesn't go to see any.

26

I didn't think I was a snob. I thought I could fit in with anyone. Provincial aristocrats, old regulars of Le Palace, hard rockers, state councilors, cops, whores, dealers, taxi drivers, students at the École normale, undocumented migrants, gigolos, socialites, down-and-outs. When your parents are upper-class junkies, you get good training. My job helps, too. But the petty bourgeoisie, I have to admit, was something I wasn't familiar with. No one told me it existed. I'd never come across it. Those are the people the likes of me never see. My classist instincts come out when I'm with her. When she says Oh shoot, when she says The little ones, when she thinks she's being chic by using formal language with me, when she takes off her shoes before walking in the house or eats her dinner early. I can't help it. I'm trying to stop. I guess that's also the point of love.

27

In the fall she invites me to her country house again. Last minute. Tomorrow, she says. She asks me to pick up a few things seeing as I'm in Paris. She says she's run out of perfume. And tea and coffee. She tells me there's no need to go to La Grande Épicerie du Bon Marché or anywhere fancy like that. She adds a smile emoji.

She says she wants me on my best behavior. I see the look in her eye, I know my role, I know the rules. That's what she invited me for. And that's why I came. I turn to face her, I put my hands on her thighs, on her neck, I kiss her. She says what she wants is just to feel pleasure. She says That feels good. Then she starts simpering, she says she shouldn't. I'm tired of constantly having to insist. I say Fine. She's disappointed, she doesn't say anything else.

One evening, outside, we're smoking cigarettes, she brings out blankets. Her children will be back soon. She puts her hand down my jeans, I stop myself from stopping her, she touches me as if she's scratching a dog's back. I wonder if that's how she touches herself. I pretend to come. I jerk her off as well. Maybe she wanted the memory of being outside in the open.

The next day, she's had too much to drink. She tells me to sleep in her bed. She says Turn around when she takes off her bra in front of me. She lies down, she looks at me, I fuck her, she comes, she turns her back to me, she falls asleep. I spend the night waiting for morning to come. I spend the night waiting for the day so I can shield my body from hers.

She never talks about love, she never says anything about me, she never makes the slightest gesture, she just spreads her legs in front of my mouth.

I meet her cousins, her aunts, her nephews. Unimaginative people with no imagination. I'm embarrassed by her lack of embarrassment.

She peels an apple with a knife, her thumb on the fruit, sliding the knife toward herself. A different language, a different childhood, a body that grasps things in a different way from mine.

Maybe she thinks that words contain real things, that reality is only there so we can find the words inside it.

Maybe she thinks she has a mistress and it's all the rage. Maybe she thinks this is what a love affair looks like. Maybe she thinks this is what courage looks like. Her name for me is liberty, sometimes she even capitalizes it.

Suddenly she wants to go for a walk, there's a child with us, she's walking so fast, she doesn't stop when he needs to tie his shoelaces, I stay with him, she doesn't slow down, we try to catch up with her, neither he nor I know the way, she carries on walking fast, I think about amok syndrome, people rushing around in a frenzy, but then there's this child, this child who's trying to follow her, trying to catch up, pushing his body forward in silence, crying in silence, before eventually he falls to the ground. I can't take any more either, she comes over to him, tells him to get up, then goes off again, she doesn't wait, she says it's getting dark, I look at the child, neither of us speak, I take his hand, we keep on walking until the end.

28

I wasn't sure if it was seedy or great. I didn't know if I should carry on. I thought Breaking up feels far too grand. There wasn't anything to break. I figured it wasn't so bad, sleeping with a married woman. Even if it wasn't that often. At least it was something. A story. A role. I got into character. In front of the mirror I scrunched up my eyes, I put on a crooked smile, a vaudeville act, I was a provincial Casanova, Aldo Maccione. I didn't really mind not having much sex, it was bad anyway.

29

Nice and short. Yes, exactly, like a boy. My body was basically made for this. What are the odds? Something in-between, a hybrid. A girl that stands as tall as a man. Nature's a beautiful thing. I know how people look at me. Everyone likes neutral. Neutral goes with everything. I think that's what Laurent liked too. He was much more my double than she is. Exactly the same size. The same size in everything. There was no one bending down to reach the other. That was one thing we had, complete equality. It's always been that way. I only ever talk to guys. I don't understand a thing women say. You always get the feeling that things are about to get out of hand. Like a boy, yes. Or a girl with short hair.

30

I don't know how it happened, how I got caught up in it all, the two of them, their business, their arrangements. I go to her place I see her husband. I call him by his first name. I kiss him on the cheek. I'm a member of the family now.

The first time I met him was before Rome. She wasn't there, we more or less bumped into each other. We could have avoided each other. We walked toward each another instead. Smiling. A slightly stern smile but genuine, too. He said I wanted to see if you really existed. I didn't say anything in reply.

After that she started bringing me back from time to time. She asked me to come in for five minutes, just like that, then it became more frequent, before or after something else, dinner or the gym, because she'd left her phone upstairs, because she needed to drop off groceries, make the kids' dinner. She brings me upstairs and observes what happens between them when I'm there.

She says He's going to ask you to stay for dinner. He asks, I say no. He hands me a glass, he says You can't say no. I don't say no. I look at him, he looks at me, I drink. I'm sure he knows. And he knows I know he knows. When I go to leave, she runs her hand over my back and stops at the nape of my neck.

One evening, he rests his arm on me and I rest mine on him. We're touching one another. On the other side of the table, in silence, in the background, she watches. He serves me wine and cheese. We're all sizing each other up as we speak. Sitting there, next to him, opposite me, she listens and watches us. Sitting there, opposite them, I look from one to the other and they both look at me, I talk, he talks, she sits in silence.

They all hate each other in this family. It's a hatred that keeps them glued to one another. But it's mostly her they hate.

Her son sends me text messages. She's asked me to talk to him about his future. It's good that you see him from time to time. He asks me to go for coffee, too. He always sits very close to me. He once asked me if I'd slept with his mother. She tells me to see him more often. She says You'll end up sleeping with him, too. She thinks that's funny.

31

I'm rich and she's poor. That's why I'm going to win. It's inevitable. The rich always win. And the poor always perish. It's not my fault. It's not my fault if it's the rich who win. It's not my fault if I'm rich. That's how I was born. It goes so far back it's in my DNA. I was born to rich parents who were born to rich parents. I'm rich without a dime. I don't have an apartment. Rich but living on ten euros per day, cigarettes included. Rich without a thing to my name, so rich that I don't care about being poor. Technically on the street but ontologically loaded. You don't need money when you're rich. You don't need other people when you're rich. You don't need anything when you're rich. It's a question of shame, and we never feel shame. Poor people are right to hate us.

32

He has a very slim build and very dark hair, he has green eyes, he's wearing a riding jacket and an old pair of corduroy pants. He comes to meet me in front of the château. Of all the cousins in the family, he and my mother were the favorites. I pull up, I park my car next to a barn, I walk across the gravel, he waits there without moving. I haven't seen him for thirty years, except last year, briefly, at his son's funeral. My uncle the archbishop said the Mass. Heroin overdose. Eighteen years old. He never smiles, he hates physical contact, he never gives me a kiss, never asks how I am. His icy eyes crinkle slightly at the sides, that's all. I remember a party they had here, the last one I came to with my mother. They had swans in the moat back then. It's a huge hunting lodge. I pick up pieces of lead shrapnel on the floor, left over from the war. This is Normandy. He says Come with me, I'll show you, he leads the way. He talks about the duchess. He wants to show me a photo of her, he says she was very beautiful.

He looks for the photo. We go through room after room. The château has been half-abandoned, but parts of it still look vaguely lived in. Some of the rooms are empty, some are full of old clutter, pieces of furniture, there's one enormous room overlooking the moat, in one bathroom a woman's things, a bottle of perfume, some creams, and on an armchair a red thong. Maybe it belongs to the woman he's been talking to on the phone for a while now, his voice bored, cold, unpleasant, and in his own way seductive. He goes into a cupboard, pulls out some liveries, gold and blue, the family colors. When he's showing me how beautiful they are, he smiles. Then there's the crockery that Louis-Philippe supposedly gifted the family for its thousandth anniversary. He tells me about the fungus that gets into everything in the château, rotting it all, filthy stuff. We find the photo in a chest of drawers. My old aunt by the sea with her two sons. She's looking away. Her hair is short, slightly curly, she's wearing some sort of dark-colored polo shirt, black or navy blue. He says men were always crazy about her but she preferred women. She had affairs, one with Arletty and another with her cousin, my grandmother's sister. She used to take morphine. She died at the age of forty-seven. I don't know if it was suicide or the morphine. She was a little crazy too, I think, but that runs in the family.

33

It's something I'd never seen before with men. Fear. The moment the eyes cloud over, the body shuts down, the tears come. That immense fear. I don't know what these tears are anymore, where they're coming from, whom they're for. One day it was so bad she doubled over with her hands over her face. I stopped midsentence, I left.

The yellow light of the stairwell and streetlights, the smell of winter and stone, the threshold. I lean against the doorway, I pull her to me by the hips, I kiss her, I let go, I start again, I stop, she looks at me, I smile, she says This girl is crazy, I don't like that sentence, I leave.

Sometimes I see her falter. I see it in those moments of tiredness when she rubs her eyes with one hand, I see it when she speaks a little too loudly, a slight shrillness in her voice, a certain agitation, a glazed look, I see it when she asks me to come over then acts like I was the only one who wanted to, I see it when her body tenses up from all the effort it takes for her to keep it all together. In those moments I see all the things about her that don't add up. I know she'll never change, the mere thought of action is alien to her. She's a woman set in her ways, adding things to things, lining up all her little boxes without ever choosing one, without ever throwing anything away. She's like those crazy people hoarding things in heaps, in their terrifying apartments you can scarcely set foot in.

One evening, she tells me she wants to get out, leave it all behind, but she doesn't know where to go. I don't say anything. In the narrow street, in the middle of the night, I kiss her, lightly, quickly, without feeling.

I could tell it surprised her the other day, when I squeezed her ribs a little too tightly. And the other time, too, when she told me I'd bitten her. I have to be more careful. That strange night when the three of us were together, he made me feel like I was complicit in a crime.

That evening, when she crosses the threshold, she's the one who stops, she's the one who looks at me, she's the one who wants to kiss me. I step back. I shake my head. She doesn't understand.

We never argue, we're always smiling. But I don't like this politeness, I'm bored of walking on eggshells. The melancholy of violence, of anger, love in all its baseness.

I swim and I don't think of anything but the movements, my body extending stretching gliding, the strokes getting cleaner, more precise, the steady rhythm of my breath.

34

The guy's in police custody, fifth arrondissement, place Maubert. He's Moroccan, he has no papers, he's practically homeless. He wears his long hair tied back in a ponytail. He admits to the theft, denies the rape. The complainant is a female doctor who lives on rue du Four. He's smart and good-looking so he charms and sweet-talks women to get money and sometimes a bed. She says he raped her. The intelligent, reasonable, rational one, the one whose body and face are in good shape, is the homeless, paper-less, recidivist Moroccan guy. The fragile, hysterical one is this white female doctor from the sixth arrondissement. It's clear as day. Even the cops agree. The prosecutor doesn't give a shit, he refers the defendant to the examining magistrate on counts of theft and rape. At the police station, I bump into another lawyer, a guy I've seen around, a strange guy, his hair's all over the place and he seems to be too, he says he's there for a case of his own, it's been going on for twenty years, something about poisoning, the secret services, he even reckons he's been chipped. Both of them are still practicing, the lawyer and the doctor. I meet my client the next day at the Palais de Justice. He spent the night there. He doesn't complain. I speak to the judge. She's not pig-headed. She can see for herself the woman isn't all there. She questions him, she charges him, but not for rape. He's remanded in custody for the counts of theft. He has fifteen convictions on his criminal record and seven months of a previous sentence left to serve. He's worried about his girlfriend who has bipolar and smokes too much cannabis and is taking care of their dog.

35

There's a certain age in childhood when you know exactly what you want. After that you're no longer sure. After that you forget. What I wanted at the age of four was simple. Short hair, boys' clothes, boys' toys, a boy's life. Everything down to swimsuits, wearing the same blue-and-white striped shorts as my male cousins in the summer. I was never self-conscious. There's no such thing at that age. The other children accepted me the way I was. I was the girl who played with the boys. I was always with them, I was their equal. That's the way it was and everyone knew it. No one would have dreamed of giving me a Barbie for my birthday. My mother and I had a frank discussion on the subject. We were in the car. She drove fast, she drove well. She told me it was OK to love girls if you're a girl. My father took me to the flea market to buy me army clothes, he taught me to tie a tie, he bought me models to build, he introduced me to Tintin and Philémon, then later Rimbaud and Malaparte, he got me into the Stones,

Johnny Cash, Arlo Guthrie. At the age of four I was homosexual. I knew full well and so did my parents. After that it kind of passed. Now it's coming back. It's as simple as that.

36

I look at her to see what a dyke looks like. She has a shaved head, she wears hooded sweaters, she rolls Lucky Strikes. There's something very gentle about her, too. In her voice, her eyes, her smile. A dyke is a girl, a real girl. She's the one who says Dyke, and I think to myself She's right. She lives with a law professor, who's sitting there next to us, working in their living room, a quiet, blond woman. I look at them to see what two women living together looks like. The apartment's quite big, not beautiful, not ugly, just normal. The girl with the shaved head is English so we speak in English. I lift my sleeve. I put my arm on the desk. She applies some gel and places the drawing on my skin. We discussed it, she suggested something, I said yes. It's beautiful but I didn't give a shit about that. I just wanted as much ink as possible under my skin. She dipped the electric needle into the ink, she set to work. A crackling sound. It didn't really hurt, it felt like a scratch, a pinch, something that makes your blood flow, like being bitten on the breast. When I left with the ink covering my arm down to my hand, my body was heavier.

37

She arrives early, she wants to have dinner right away. Eating is important to her. She likes to comment on her food. I've made pasta. Simple, greasy. A dish for her. I bought her wine of course because she always drinks. I pull back my armchair and watch her. She eats, she talks, I don't know what about. I'm not hungry. I'm disgusted by it all tonight, her body, her life, her words. I smoke. She can't even hear my silence. She wipes her mouth, she lies down, she spreads her arms. I fuck her because that's what she wants. Without undressing, without making an effort, because she can't tell the difference either way. When she leaves I throw the rest of the dinner out with her present. Merry Christmas.

Part Two

1

In the street and in the metro, I look at girls. Their breasts, their asses, their cunts, the curves of their waistlines. I imagine how they smell, I imagine seeing that look in their eye, I imagine their sighs, what pleasure would do to their faces. I wonder what I would do to them if they were mine. Not all of them. Not necessarily the prettiest. But the ones who have something about them, a thing only girls have. I have a radar for it now. It's something a lot of girls have, that thing, if you know how to spot it. I don't think I ever looked at men like that, before. I don't remember. I don't think you can look at men and women in the same way. Sexually, I mean. I look at girls and I can tell, they sense my eyes on them. I can see they feel my desire. And it all becomes so easy. The fear just disappears.

2

We've barely seen each other since we separated. We communicate via text. As little as possible. I went over to drop off some stuff for our son. His place isn't very big but it's bigger than mine. And even more of a dump. I'd never have been able to live with a neat freak, anyway. He's acting normal for once. We have a drink. That champagne of his, extradry, phosphate-free, he explains. He has little quirks like that, his wines and his shirts. We go and pick up some pizzas. He says he likes my hair short. What I hadn't anticipated was him kissing me and us sleeping together. I didn't think I had anything to worry about. I thought he had a girlfriend as well. Maybe it's because at some point I asked him whether he thought we were happier now that we're not together anymore. I don't know what came over me, talking about happiness like that out of nowhere. I should have stopped him. But instead I did what I used to do. All the same movements I used to do. It wasn't great, obviously.

I didn't stay over. He wanted to see me again the next day. We got coffee. We talked about something else. In a certain sense it would have been simpler if it could've worked. But I don't think that's possible.

3

Once a year, or every two years, Henry calls me and we go for a drink. He doesn't see my father now but he still sees me. I like his creased shirts, the smell of stale tobacco on him, his pasty-white hands. Something I've always thought is that he seems to have managed to extricate himself from life, just the way I want to. Minus the drugs. Back in the day when he used to hang around with my father and Robert, he would always end up getting kicked out of apartments for not paying rent, crashing at friends' places, juggling things around. Things seem to have been going better for the last ten years or so. Every now and then he'll sell a painting or publish something. He doesn't seem to attach much importance to work, he just does it to prevent catastrophe. I think that's what I like, the idea of catastrophe, the fact that he's always on the verge of it and yet manages to keep it at bay.

I was in court when he sent me the text. He was having lunch with his daughter in the neighborhood. I might as well join them, he said. The case was bullshit. I got there slightly late. He'd already left. She waited for me. I didn't know her very well, really. She was drinking a Coke, she had short, dark hair and very pale skin, she was wearing a jacket with a fur collar, dark sunglasses, red lipstick. She'd just returned from New York where she lived for ten years. Her name is Albertine but everyone calls her Albert. She's a real girl though, Albert. Her mother was a dancer at the Crazy Horse. Makes sense.

I hadn't seen her since childhood. Her childhood, not mine, there's a fifteen-year age gap between us. But I'd seen her on Facebook. It was when she posted something like Girls Do It Much Better that I knew. Before, she was normal, she was like me, she was straight. She posted selfies. She turned out sexy. She liked it that way. So did I, obviously.

She's so small. That's the first thing I thought when I walked over to her table, she was still so small and she still had that black, piercing stare she had when she was eight years old and I saw her clinging to her father's legs, silent, strange, immune to smiles. She was wearing a T-shirt under her jacket that showed off her small, round breasts when she leaned toward me for a lighter. That's one of the things I liked about her, that steeliness.

4

She says she remembers me leaning against a door frame. She says I have the same expression too, head tilted down slightly, the same disinclination to talk. She says she's been keeping up with my life through her father, that she was surprised when she heard I got married and had a child, she says she always knew. She's come back to live in Paris. I don't really understand what she does, whether she works. Maybe she really was thinking about me while she was living in New York. She did send me an invitation for an opening, she said it in English, *opening*, I remember now. The invite was beautiful. It was a Polaroid of a naked woman, you couldn't see her face, she was wearing a red bodice. I kept it for a long time.

What's all this supposed to mean? We don't know each other. I'm fifteen years older than her. It wouldn't make any sense. She says That's just how it is. She smiles. I look at her. I think about that Polaroid again.

5

We had lunch at a café, we bought cigarettes, Mentos, two scratch cards. She said yes when I asked her to come up. I have tea. She's sitting across the room in an old armchair. She's wearing white, ripped jeans. I look at her knees, the pale skin of her knees, I like that they're muscly on the sides. She's so far away. There's the armchair, her sweaters, the fox fur hiding her chin. She doesn't speak much, she's looking at me. We're both slightly uncomfortable. I know what she came here for. I know I'm going to kiss her. The whole thing is terrifying. I need something to lean on, I place my hands on her knees, I tilt toward her, I lean in, I kiss her. We're trying each other out. I'm kneeling down to be at her level. I have to get used the smell of her perfume, her eyes so close to mine, her head in my hand. I didn't touch her skin under her clothes that day. I thought about how soft her breasts would be. I don't know how long it went on, five minutes, half an hour. By the time we stopped it was almost night.

6

At night she sleeps with her body pressed up to mine, her arm around me, when I turn over she turns over too and wraps her arm around me again. When I wake up I see her tiny hand on my body. I wonder how she can sleep so close to someone she doesn't know. In the morning, naked on my bed or wearing nothing but my sweater, far too big for her, eyes still closed, a sulky look about her, she runs her hand over the nape of my neck, then my stomach, my breasts, she says Do you have to go? In my bed, the smell of her, the warmth of her body in the morning. I shower, put on jeans, I leave, she goes back to sleep.

Hours go by, they keep on passing, gently, gradually, slowly. I don't care about pleasure, what I'm interested in is desire, a desire I'd never known before, this never-ending desire.

Those pale days, the pale light, her pale skin, the pale sky tinged with pink at five o'clock when I know she's on her way, when the hands of the clock lean toward her. I don't think I'd known anything like it before, this softness of hers combined with something else, something slightly closed off and steely, something that suggests she's incapable of lying.

A scalding-hot shower before she arrives and the clean, sweet smells of our bodies and her skin so white and so soft it looks powdered and her face frozen by the winter air, and she catches her breath—Five flights of stairs, Jesus Christ!—her black coat, her fox fur, I even like her sneakers. She says I'm making you dinner, I like cooking for you. She says Cool, she says Gorgeous, her voice clear and sharp, her body upright, her shoulders square.

And even her ears, and her fingers in my mouth, and the hours and the hours, and Your boobs are amazing, and I bite her neck, and my tongue on her tongue, and her clean-shaven, delicate skin, and her on top, how light she feels, her frame, her waist, bending in two beneath my hands, the dimples on her hips—Are you tired? Yes, no— and her tongue on my nipples, gentle as anything, and her sighs, and then—Are you thirsty?—and on and on, every day, in my bed.

Every evening, every night, she comes over, she sleeps, she's there. She says Shall I order something in for when you get back? She leaves me a note. She takes one of my sweaters. Something cold, something sweet, something shimmery, as good as the heroin my old man used to take, her old man too, that's how she refers to them, I have to admit, it suits them.

She says she already loved me when she was eight. She says she never stopped thinking about me. I wonder if she's just telling me that to make me happy. Or to make herself happy. She likes telling stories. I don't trust everything she says. But maybe she did love me as a child.

I made the move but it was she who wanted it. I wasn't going to say no to what she saw in me.

7

A woman's body is made to be touched and tasted, a woman is made to be fucked. Breasts are made for hands to feel, an ass is made to be pressed up against, a cunt is made for a face to go down on, to breathe in the scent, to slip in the tongue, the fingers, to suck and to taste, that fucking sweet taste. No man can compete with that. I understand people who go to whores. For the first time, I feel it like a sting, all the violence of desire. The desire for women's bodies. The things they say, too, but maybe that doesn't matter. The same with their faces, deep down I feel indifferent about them, except for maybe the mouth. No man could ever have that effect on me. But maybe I'm just saying that because it's her. I didn't know sex could be this good. I didn't know it could be this important. She says the same thing. I don't know if she means it or if she's just saying it to make me happy. It's important to be polite. Albert makes me hard. She and I are only fucking. But I'm wondering if maybe I never knew love before.

8

I saw Agnès. I told her about Albert. She asked me if it was going well. I said yes. She asked me if it was going to change things between us. It was the first time she'd ever said *us*. I said it would change things somewhat, yes. I could see her hesitation, I could see her calculating the twenty-five-year age gap between her and Albert, I could see her imagining what it was like. She didn't ask for any explanations, she didn't yell at me, she smiled. I put on a sorry face.

9

I chose Florence at random, either for the price or the flight times. We had to make a stop in Bologna because of the wind. It was cold and gray. It was Italy but it didn't look like Italy. We took a bus on the autostrada, Albert ate a Twix and fell asleep, it rained.

The hotel is the kind of place you might find charming if you're English or American and not made of money, the room is big, the bed too. She's sitting down, my hand is stroking her over her panties, I feel her warmth on the tips of my fingers, I'm barely touching her, we're barely moving, I slip the tips of my fingers inside, I listen to her breathing, I'm the one touching her but it feels like I'm the one who's going to come, did I know before that desire could be something as big as this? Afterward we go for dinner and even the food seems sexual. She kisses me in the street. It makes me feel a little uncomfortable but I don't feel strongly about it either way. I have to bend down a lot to kiss her,

I think about the word, to *bend*, somehow it makes the movement sound exaggerated. She stands on tiptoe.

We go out for a walk, to look for a restaurant, a café, we go out because we're hungry, because we want to get some air, see some daylight, the sun, the rain, it's raining like crazy, she slips her hand into my pocket, we look for the restaurant we went to yesterday, it really was good, the GPS app sends us all over the place, we push open church doors, I stroke her breasts on the staircase, she wants to kiss me in front of the monsignors, we test almond creams on our wrists, even my fingers touching her shoulder sends a shiver of pleasure through my body.

Then there are the nights, the afternoons, the mornings. Getting to know her body, it's so light and supple, her body, soft and pale, I didn't know a woman could be this handsome. And all the other moments as well, all the shyness of lovers of two days, we don't show it of course, that would be gay.

What do you do with all your desire? Show me. And how do you deal with fear and tenderness and hatred and boredom? Show me. When my nose grazes your skin and your eyes meet mine, are we capable of all the things we say we are? I like you like this, cynical, fraternal. Don't hold my hand, don't tell me you love me. I bite my lips to keep them sealed, bashfully I lick your breasts.

We were in it for better, right from the start, because what comes next is always for worse, and as far as we were concerned for worse could go fuck itself. Tragedy was always part of the deal, I think.

10

I told my son. That I liked girls, that I liked Albert. It was very simple. I asked him if he already had an inkling. He said yes but he wasn't sure. He says he likes Albert. He says she's funny. She came for dinner a couple of times on the weeks when I had him. She never stayed over on those nights. Afterward he was very tender with me. He came into the kitchen to give me a kiss. He said he loved me. We never really say those kinds of things, he and I. He talked about himself, his friends, his life. We went to get a grenadine in the café downstairs. We went for a walk. It was a nice day. We went to the florist. He chose some Persian buttercups. He asked if I could put them in his bedroom.

11

What I like about her is her ethic, her relationship with the world excites me. Albert doesn't work. She spends her whole life in bed. She thinks. Or sleeps. She doesn't need to justify herself by saying she read Hegel as a child. When it comes to money, she gets by. Always on the cusp of ruin. Finally someone living in my world. One day she asked me What class do we belong to? I said We're the relegated upper class. Double or quits, darling. I'm not gay. Me too, me neither. Bite my breasts. Not homo, but sexual. You're alright, I guess. Let's call each other by our family names. I can't believe how soft your skin is. Don't change your perfume. I wasn't going to, darling.

12

He took a shower, so did I. He wears Vétiver, I wear Habit Rouge. I made coffee. He was sleeping when we arrived last night. He says How's the kid? Everything in order? I say Fine, everything's fine. We talk about politics. I never smoke in front of my father. He looks at the clock. He says Where the hell is she? He's waiting for the nurse to bring him his Subutex. Yesterday on the phone I said Hi, I'm a lesbian now, do you remember Henry's daughter? Can I come this weekend? I never did find out why he fell out with Henry. I go back to my room. Albert wakes up. We fuck. She says I made more noise than usual. I doubt it. It's a beautiful day. She eats reblochon for breakfast. It's things like that that make me love her. I show her the concierge's house nearby. She says That would be perfect for us. I say yes. I know we'll never do it but it doesn't matter.

The important thing is to say yes. I find a photo of her mother, pregnant with her, when they came to visit thirty years ago. She doesn't speak to her mother anymore. My father doesn't speak to us either, he doesn't join us for breakfast. But he never speaks and he never has breakfast so I can't tell if he's sulking or not. We take a walk in the vineyard. The woman who's vaguely taking care of my father turns up out of nowhere. She's eighty-five. She's never left the countryside and all she does is talk about the chemist's widow who she knows from the Rotary Club and Madame Plandu and all the problems she's having with her new daughter-in-law. She smiles. She tells Albert she needs to cook lots of nice dinners for me because I'm too skinny. I'm not skinny but it doesn't seem essential to point that out at this moment in time. I like her. Her name is Fanny. She takes us to the station in her battered old Volvo. Me in the front. Albert in the back. She takes a photo of me wearing my father's old jacket. I look at the road, I smile. The next day my sister tells me my father is distraught. That feels like a very strong word to describe the kinds of feelings we generally have in this family. I call my father. He says The poor child, what must he think? He says I could do better. Albert doesn't have a degree.

13

She's very good with her tongue. And her fingers. Just thinking about it makes me want her. Sometimes we fuck softly, gently, there's something about it that feels like perfect equality, completely sexual but almost child-like at the same time because it's so pure. Sometimes I fuck her more like a man. I don't remember how it started. It was her ass that brought the whole thing about. Before I was happy going down on her, using my hands, touching her, smelling her, slipping my tongue or finger in. That day, I was behind her, my cunt up against her ass, my hand on hers. I could see she liked it. So I really went for it. She came hard. It can go on for hours. We can make each other come ten times over. The whole thing is mind-blowing. Nobody has ever fucked me like that. She says I'm a boy and a girl at the same time. We're still too shy for accessories. It's all pure innocence.

14

It's a shame he's dead. I can picture the scene, the pink-and-white striped tablecloth, Ludivine setting the dishes out in her blue-and-white striped blouse with a little white apron over the top because it's lunchtime, a servant's apron like you see in the theater, guinea fowl green beans sautéed potatoes or rib steak green beans sautéed potatoes, and I have to say I loved that food that was always the same and the tablecloth that was always the same and Ludivine who was always the same, she was even Black, Ludivine, how chic, a Black servant for white people, even if it wasn't intentional, and my grandmother would always make a point of saying she was pretty and that she herself had Indian blood and maybe even Chinese blood but in hindsight it hardly seems likely for her to have had Chinese blood, but anyway, I can picture the scene, I would wait for everyone to be served and then I'd tell them, just to piss my grandfather off if nothing else because no one in the family would ever dare to piss my grandfather off because they all desperately needed his greatness even though he was a piece of shit, in my opinion, or at least I could never stand the man, a physical repulsion, because he was small, stout, and short-legged, because he nibbled his potatoes between his front teeth, because his body stayed vertical, straight as a ramrod, when he swam, because he never stood up when a woman entered the room, because he didn't know how to drive, because he believed in his own importance, because it was grotesque, all of it, the whole spectacle, because he was nothing but a hick, it was clear from all his gestures, all his indignation, and I think it's hilarious that people admired him for it, as if they were the Kennedys when actually the man had no style and was nothing but a huge embarrassment, and don't even get me started on their morals, their shitty little morals, but you get the picture, it's all part of the same thing, so anyway I would have said to them Grand-father dearest, I have something I want to say, my dear, paternal family, sitting there with your sticks up your asses, because even if the aristocrats on Mom's side were all crazy and practically illiterate, at least my good old aunt was sleeping with Arletty and nobody gave a fuck because it wasn't as bad as watching their châteaux go up in flames and their money vanish into thin air, and anyway all they cared about was that drop of Jewish blood floating around in there somewhere, even though they raked in millions because of it, Darling, do you think I have a Jewish nose? and anyway on Dad's side we have a rabbi in the family which of course is a little embarrassing but now we're all nice and white we can pretend it's chic, so anyway where was I, my dear, anally retentive family, and I insist on the *dear* because they're honestly quite nice a lot of the time, except for the big man and all his bullshit, which I found particularly hilarious the day I walked in on him sitting there in the bath like an idiot, the minister with his dick out, floating in the tepid water, even if I absolutely love having his fucking last name, though it's not as chic as Mom's name but I actually think it's more fun to have the hick name that everyone thinks is chic, thanks Grandpapa, don't mind if I do, and anyway it would be a nightmare having an aristocratic particle in my name, you just can't go around with a name like that nowadays, my first name is bad enough, but back to my point, yes, sorry, ting ting ting, knife on the glass, I've got some news, I am simply ecstatic to announce, ecstatic as in ecstasy as in the climax of the story, please listen carefully and make sure you've swallowed your mouthful, grab a glass of water and keep your medication to hand, Ludivine, fetch the smelling salts! Do I have your attention? Is everyone listening? I eat girls' cunts out and suck their nipples and I slip my fingers up their cute little asses because Grandpa, Granny, aunts and uncles, Ludivine dearest, I am a dyke. Now, Ludivine, how about that salad? The problem is, no one has servants these days.

15

With everyone else, it was simple. If anyone asked me if I had a boyfriend, I told them I had a girlfriend. I don't think anyone gives a shit. Some people even congratulated me. But with Laurent, I'm not so sure. He seemed fine at first. Then he started acting weird. I think it's because he saw me in the street with Albert. Because if I want to kiss Albert in the street, I kiss her in the street, I take her by the waist, I pull her toward me, I take her face in my hands and I kiss her if I want to kiss her, in my heteronormative neighborhood, the sixth arrondissement of Paris, or anywhere else for that matter. And that's when it all started going downhill. He told me to get a grip on myself. He brought up our son. I didn't reply. I think he's jealous. That was the first time he'd seen me with someone since we split up. And besides my girlfriend is better than his.

16

Yesterday I threw out some skirts, a dress, some heels, some bags. She said it was strange to think of me wearing them. I never wore them much. I wasn't interested in the kind of power accorded to women for wearing that uniform. At the age of ten I was building models, at the age of twelve I was shooting rifles, and all it took to get Laurent into bed was a pair of Vans and a moped. It never stopped me from being a girl, but a girl on my own terms. After his affair with the intern, I tried being more feminine, I tried wearing heels, stockings, and all the rest of it. I tried to play the part. I saw what kind of power it gives you. I saw how men looked at me. It was easy. I even tried fucking Laurent like that. I tried to be a bit of a whore. He told me to walk around, dressed in a bra and stockings, while he got his dick out. He wanted me to jerk him off with my Louboutins. He stuck his cock into the garter. He said You're costing me a fortune, you know. He'd look at himself in the mirror while he was fucking me from behind. I could see his legs, they were shorter than mine, I would lower myself down to make it easier for him. We never really clicked sexually, he and I. Or maybe in the beginning, but I don't remember. In the end he wanted to fuck all the time but he had to jerk himself off to come. Sometimes I could get off but it was quite depressing. There were a couple of guys after him. But apart from that one guy who drove me crazy when he touched me that time in Le Baron, nothing really stands out, to be honest. With Albert, everything is simple. She tells me I'm beautiful, beautiful in my own field, this combination of boy and girl. That's something I didn't know before.

17

And then winter again. And those afternoons. And those nights. And Paris. Her sighs and her silences, her putting Honey Loops in my mouth. Lie on your stomach. Do you want to come to Sweden with me? I don't know what's better, her mouth on my breast or my mouth on hers. When she kisses me in the kitchen, when she lifts up my sweater, her hands, her mouth, the powdery taste of her lipstick. Her soft skin, her puppy-like smell. When she says You, in your jeans, topless.

Her kisses in the morning. Her warmth in the night. Her taste in the night. I seek out the things beneath her tongue that have rotted in her since the night before, a taste of her death, in her I look for my own violence.

One day, I won't want her or she won't want me and it'll all be over and that's the reason we have to keep going from city to city and her skin and her mouth and Where are we going next weekend and Tomorrow afternoon come over to my place and get in my bed and after that we'll go to a café and after that we'll go back to bed until there's no more saliva left in my mouth and my body's so tired it can't take anymore. Her, until I black out. Like a dose without restraint and measure, sweetness and desire, all that exists is today. Who will be the first to leave? Who will be the first to get scared?

And if I hold her in my arms, it's not for my pleasure, it's to understand how she deals with reality and twists it with me, how far we can twist it together, how far we can cheat death.

18

My father, that fucker, he asked me what I saw in her. I should have told him he hasn't seen her naked. That he doesn't know anything about her and the way she loves me. When it comes down to it, he never likes anyone we bring home. The guys are all pussies and my girlfriend's not good enough. He's the mother-in-law from hell. I should have gone all in with the locker room talk, I should have stood tall with my thumbs in pockets and told him she's a fireball in the sack and that he's not the one fucking girls anymore, it's over for him and it's my turn now.

The other day I went for a drink with one of Albert's exes. There were a few of us there, it wasn't planned. He's a huge guy with enormous hands. I looked at his hands and I looked at mine. I wondered if he was thinking the same thing. I wondered if he had the same images going through his head as he ordered his whiskey and I was sipping on my Coke. We didn't speak about her. We were very polite. Thoughtful, even. I think that must be why. I didn't feel jealous. It was the same with Agnès's husband, I couldn't be jealous of either of them, we weren't in competition. They didn't seem to be jealous, either.

I watch her like a voyeur. I watch her when she's sleeping, when she's getting dressed, when she's talking to me and I'm not listening, when she's making dinner, when she's reading, when she's talking to other people, when she's putting on her makeup, when she looks at herself in the mirror. Sometimes I see the ugly side of her, too. I'm saving those images for when we don't love each other anymore.

19

Do you want to be my plus-one? I never go to these kinds of events alone. But with her, why not? Black-tie evenings, Sir and Madam, the Legion of Honor ceremony. Madam and Madam. She leaves no room for ambiguity, she takes me by the arm, she wants to see how far she can go before I get embarrassed, she wants me to kiss her in front of all the old people. She was happy about going to the lawyers' ball. I wore a tuxedo. She wore a lot of makeup. Then she said I wasn't paying her enough attention. She doesn't like me talking to other people. She sat there sulking. We ended up leaving.

She wants me to get a divorce, she wants to get married, forever and a day. Either with me or somebody else. She dreams of having a house in the country, a bougie apartment in the city, she dreams of having stability and she wonders if she'll be able to stick with it. She dreams of finding someone who has only ever loved her, someone who will love her forever. She dreams of being able to love someone else forever. She covers her ears when I say it's OK to let things die. She dreams of being saved.

This morning, she was talking about the summer, a house in Spain. There's no point telling her we'll never last until then.

20

She was moaning about the sofa, she said I should buy a bed and a proper comforter as well. I said Yes yes OK but I didn't do anything about it. She's found an apartment. I go to hers now. I sleep there every night when I don't have my son. I feel like I'm too tall for her tiny apartment. I feel like I'm going to knock over her cactus plants every time I move. I feel like she's going to yell at me if I go out for a coffee. In the beginning I would spend whole days at her place. Then it was only the night. Now I can't sleep anymore. I get up and wait in the kitchen for morning to come. I always take a book with me when I go to hers, in anticipation. I leave when she wakes up. I tell her I have things to do.

21

When I get in the water I think about how I'm going to leave her. And then I calm down. I feel calm again. The certainty that it's not for me to choose. When I climb the last few stairs and I know she's waiting for me I wonder how I can stop her from noticing that I don't love her anymore. And then she's there and I love her again. I don't do anything. Nothing apart from being there. Loving her when I love her and otherwise swimming. She hates me going swimming. I think that's why she always wants to fuck so late at night. So that I won't swim in the morning and I'll stay with her instead. She says my morning crawl represents all the things she's not capable of. I don't know what she means.

22

I'm not mad at her, how could I be? It's so touching when
she hates me. Maybe I'm only saying that because she's so
small. One night she hit me, she said she had some kind
of cramp. She thought I was seeing that girl again, the
model, she started talking about Laurent. She's jealous,
she's stalking me on Facebook. She doesn't go as far as following me or rifling through my phone. At least I don't
think so. She gets on my case about everything, about
nothing. At night she'll let out a sigh then start crying.
She wants me to be hers and hers only. She doesn't want
me to go anywhere. She wants me to get my nipple
pierced. She says it would turn her on. She wants blood,
proof, trophies. It's normal, she's a girl. She doesn't have
kids yet so she can't take it out on them. I'm innocent,
purity itself, the definition of Good. My secret is being
selfish. Completely and utterly selfish. For my own good
and for the good of everyone else. The same goes for my
son. It's normal, I'm not his mother, I'm his father, and

fathers have no fear, they don't have this need to be loved by their children, so they leave them the fuck alone and let them grow up. Laurent is his mother. He's doing a wonderful job of it. Though he's a bit of a mess at times. He really should tidy up his place and make a bit more effort when it comes to cooking, maybe bake a cake for his kid now and then. Really, he'd better get his shit together or else he's going to turn his son into a fag. This is all because of Albert. It's because of her I'm talking shit. She's draining me, she's killing me. But when I manage to get some sleep, when she isn't there, I tell myself that there's no man who'd be capable of loving me that much.

23

I'm so scared of not being able to come. It's terrifying how much it terrifies me. I don't know what I'd do with the emptiness. That's why you have to be tough, you have to keep your body strong. To get through the fear. Fear of desire, fear of love, all the fears. Then everything will be OK.

24

She says she wants to hurt me. That's all right, darling, I wouldn't expect anything less, honey bun. I've got the best position, the *M* in S & M, I'm the customer, the object, the one who benefits from the other person's violence, just wait and see, soon you'll realize you never knew me either. Who is the strongest? How far are you brave enough to go? Go on, show me. We don't need costumes, we don't need accessories. Just her fingers pinching me a little harder, her teeth biting down a little more than before. And then waiting for the next move. She doesn't say a word, she doesn't smile, she looks at me, I look at her. I observe her hatred. In admiration. Please do not disturb. A girl is a beautiful thing. A girl is not sweetness but rage.

25

How long can we go without breathing? It feels like there's no more air. It's the heat beneath the rooftops, I don't know how long it's been since I got a good night's sleep. Maybe it's no longer desire that keeps us up so late, maybe it's fear or boredom or anger. I don't think she's sleeping either, or maybe in the morning when I'm not there. At night I hear coming and going, but I don't know if it's real or if it's only a dream. Will you be here tomorrow? I'm tired too, I'm so tired.

The experience of the self, of the other, coming and going, presence followed by breakdown. Stripped down in front of you, what would I know how to do? Who would I know how to be? Would I know how to be there? Would I want you? And would we want each other? It's not an option to lie. Celebration and disaster. In their closest, truest form. And our capacity to be open to both, to accept them, let them in.

She says the words *intoxicating, strapping, penetrating*. She told me, much later maybe, that I was the one who showed her what it's like to love someone like her. She said My God how awful! She laughed.

But there's nothing I can do for her. And maybe that's why I love her, and the violence and the anger and the silence of her desire, and that's why I never say a word.

She tells me she wants to host orgies, chic ones. But she's never been to an orgy except for one time in New York just to see and she thought the whole thing was seedy. I like her wide mouth, the pale lips. I like it when she says It's crazy how much I like you, It's crazy how much I want you, It's crazy how much I crave you, and when I make her come by barely touching her and when she tells me to hurt her and when, without asking, without so much as a glance or a smile, she unbuttons my jeans and goes down on me and when we're walking through Paris and she puts her hand in my pocket and when she's angry and she laughs and says I still think you're cool, you know, even when you're being a moody little bitch.

Do we love each other, or kill each other? She doesn't speak, I don't speak, we don't tell lies, I watch her go from one to the other, I watch myself go from one to the other.

I'm getting more and more tired and I want an empty fridge and I want to flick my ash into empty cans and I want to be in my own mess and dirt and I don't want to speak to anyone in the evening and I want to swim in the morning and I want to sleep, more than anything I want to sleep. I love her and I hate her. But maybe she's the one who stopped loving me first.

I want us to take each other seriously. And if I want to touch you, I want to be able to touch you without saying a thing. And if I kill you, I want to do it without growing weak. And I want to tell you if I desire you, or tell you that I don't, and do so looking you straight in the eye and I want you to do the same for me and when you do, I want to be able to hear it without flinching.

26

I got my Rolex back. I gave her back her cross. That's how we ended it. Before, I didn't believe in that kind of thing. Her moon incantations and all the rest of it. But there were things going on that weren't quite right. I lost my keys, I kept breaking things. There was the thing with the goldfish, too. We went to pick it up from the garden center, my son and I took an Autolib', it was a big thing. I sensed right away it was going to end badly. There was something weird about that fish. Technically, I can't say it died, the body was never found. The bowl was there, with the sad little shell at the bottom, but the fish was gone. I looked in the shell, I looked on the table, on the floor, the sofa, the armchair, everywhere. Nothing. Probably a cat that came in through the window. Still, it was a lot. So I went to see Antoine. A friend who sells watches. I asked him to take mine. Exchange it for another one. He did. The '69 model. It had only just come in stock.

27

I decided to go and see my father. That's why I'm in the train. Fanny told me she found a shard of glass next to him the other day when she went over to see him. The neighbors called, he'd fallen. He told her he kept the shard of glass so he could kill himself but he hadn't been able to pluck up the courage. He was holding on to it just in case. Obviously we don't think he'll ever pluck up the courage. She had to get him down once when he tried to hang himself in the barn but I'm not sure how serious the whole thing was. It feels a little stupid coming here because we more or less said everything we had to say yesterday over the phone. I don't know what I'm doing here. I'll find some old photo, post it on Instagram. Maybe the one of the opium box. I didn't buy a ticket. I didn't get caught. He's asked me to buy whiskey five times in the past twenty-four hours. Little bottles. I ended up buying a big bottle and filling up five of the empty bottles I found in the bin. There would have been no point in saying no. He'd have called a taxi to go to Super U. He can't ride a bike anymore and he can't walk either. So he blows all his money on taxis. Ten euros for five hundred yards. He doesn't buy food anymore anyway. Ever. He drinks protein shakes for old people. I counted the empty bottles in the kitchen, there were fifty-seven. Hazelnut, coffee, vanilla. They look like little milkshakes. Six hundred calories per bottle. I thought Seeing as I've come all this way to be bored shitless in shitty Touraine, seeing as I've managed to fleece the SNCF and get a free train ride, we might as well have a little talk, he and I. Especially as he might be about to croak. Especially as I wasn't in the mood for chitchat. Empty words, politeness, silence. It's not our style to have a talk. But it would be a shame not to try it once in our lives, as father and daughter. I decided to treat him like a living person. A living person you can hit. Not a dead person you just smile at. He obviously sensed what was coming. He's not completely stupid yet. Acting the confused old man doesn't work on me. He tried to make me feel sorry for him. He said I'm waiting to die so I can leave you the house. You have to see the house to understand how comical the statement was. I laughed. I said In the meantime, what's the problem? What's your problem with me? With me seeing girls? He said I can't explain. At that point I almost dropped it, I almost left him there all bundled up in the living room armchair, wrapped up to his eyeballs in his pea coat even though it was hot outside, to go and smoke in the garden or read in my room. Because I'm a coward, too. But then I thought about love, real love, not the type that gets scared at the slightest whiff of shit. And I was fed up with the little techniques he uses to stop anyone from ever asking him anything. So I said And what about Mom? We loved her so much, you and I, didn't we? Let's talk about Mom shall we? Don't you think she ever tried it? Didn't she ever mention it? Not even a little threesome? What about all those beautiful friends she loved so much? And what about that woman who owned the restaurant on rue Bonaparte, the one who always discreetly said hello to her, the one she said she met a long time ago at a girls' club? No? Doesn't ring a bell? And what about you? Has it never crossed your mind? Have you never thought about it? He didn't reply, he said that he wasn't well, that he needed to get treatment, that he was even thinking of going back to Sainte-Anne Hospital. Then he started talking about leaving us the house again. But it's too small for me and my sister, who gets by as best she can in her little life with everything planned out, her little life that's no easier than mine, her fears that are no less significant than mine, and anyway what the fuck do I care about this fucking house? He closed his eyes. He pretended to be sleeping. I looked at him and wondered whether it was the drugs that killed off his last brain cells or if deep down he'd always been like that, just like his father, bourgeois, uptight, and I wondered if maybe I'd been wrong about him all these years, thinking he was free just because he spent his life running away from all the things that he hated and I hated too. When he opened his eyes I realized. I realized he wasn't suffering. I realized that, for the first time in his life, he hated me. Because I was talking to him as an equal, a rival, a son, perhaps. And he was the one losing, of course he was, because that's the way it goes, because he's old and I'm young. I realized that the lying was over, the kind of lies you tell to children, the kind of lies you tell out of pity. I didn't think it was a big deal. It seemed normal to me. I thought about the day my son told me that he couldn't stand a single thing I do and how much I loved him in that moment. My dad took his sleeping pills. He went to bed. I ate a pack of miniwieners in front of the TV, straight from the packet, dipped in a pot of mustard. I thought it was strange how everyone was suddenly hating me these days. I didn't mind. I told myself that was another thing about the girls, they help me to see other people. To see that it takes so little. That it all rests on so little.

Part Three

1

I found out that Albert had gone back to the girl she was seeing before me. It wasn't my finest moment but I got back in touch with Agnès. It was easy. I knew she'd reply. I sent her a text. She suggested going for a drink. I met her by the court. She didn't know what to say. She seemed a little uncomfortable. She said It's funny, I was just thinking about you. She looked better than I remembered. Maybe because she had a tan. I walked her to her bike. She got on, I was standing in front of her, holding her front wheel between my legs, she put her hands on the handlebars, I put my hands over hers, I kissed her. I knew she was afraid of being seen. So I made it last. She didn't protest. We slept together again, at my place, the next day. It was bad, obviously. I felt pretty lousy. Like when you can't sleep and you get up in the middle of the night to eat something cold in the light of the open fridge. I went for a swim.

2

I'd get my hands done but it might make things complicated for work. There's a photo of a transvestite hanging
above the shelves, heavily made up, grave expression, beautiful. Transvestites always make me think of my mother.
Her boyish body, smooth, tough, the epitome of femininity,
her furs, her jewelry, her heels, my mother the model, my
mother the aristocrat, my strange and serious mother. It's a
good thing she's dead. We loved her too much, my father
and I. It wasn't healthy. I wanted something ordinary. A
heart, an anchor, anything. Tattoos aren't meant to be beautiful. They should look like graffiti on the back of a toilet
door. I would have bought a tattoo gun and done it myself
but it wouldn't have been the same. I like the idea of someone else bending over my body to do it. She gave me a
pinup on my shoulder. Slightly ugly, dirty, tragic. I went
home thinking that aside from fillings, tattoos are the only
thing you can be more or less sure of taking to the grave.

3

That night, I forgot to kiss her. I almost apologized. I've gotten out of the habit. She didn't say anything.

I don't want to know about sadness, love, boredom, I don't want to hear about all that banal, abstruse clutter. I only want to believe in actions, Agnès's messages, Albert's silence. I'll take what's there. I no longer have mercy.

Every morning at the swimming pool, I look in the mirror before going through the showers, I check my body, the bones, the muscles, the tendons, something obscure yet distinct holding everything together. A girl there laughs and calls me Nikita and I smile back at her.

The desire is still there with her, at the café, outside, where nothing can happen. I put my hand on the collar of her jacket, I squeeze her knee, I stroke the back of her leg with the palm of my hand over the rough material of her jeans.

Is it happiness or boredom, consolation or sadness? I don't think about it, I don't give anything a name. She's happy to go along with it, there's no need to split hairs.

No sooner have we started seeing each other again than she's back to her old ways, simpering when I invite her over. But I've been here a hundred times before.

She says I had a sex dream, kind of. I ask if I was in the dream, she says yes. I wonder what she means by *kind of*. I remember that desire can be something other than just a dream and that love can just be tenderness.

It's easy loving her less. She even said she thinks it's beautiful, what she and I have going on right now. I think that put me off, like thousands of other things about her that put me off. Still, there's something sweet about the days we're spending together. But now, when I kiss her, the taste that's left in my mouth is the taste of all the things I know about her.

I wonder if it's ever occurred to her that there are other ways of touching each other than the way we always do it, I wonder how she jerks guys off, how she sucks their dicks. I think about the lover she told me about, the one who looks like me, the one she was never able to make love to. Those are her words. *Make love.* She says she's always loved love. I wonder if she's ever thought of a lover as another possible life. When she says the word *love*, I see all the little wrinkles around her little mouth, I imagine all the stories she tells herself when she's in her bedroom, next to the photos of the kids.

She asked me to show her a photo of Albert on my phone but then the topic of conversation changed and I never answered, I never showed her. Sometimes she refuses to say her name, the other day she said It feels like there's always a third person there. Then she said it's good that we can talk about these things openly, that she didn't think it was possible. Maybe that's when she also said What we have is something mixed. She starts theorizing, she says Sometimes we lay together, sometimes we don't.

She wants to introduce me to a guy she likes, a guy my age, who probably doesn't like her in that way. I ask her why, what she's hoping for, what she imagines will happen. She says I don't know.

I'm ashamed on her behalf, for all her infidelities. I want to tell the men she's cheated on with me It really wasn't all that.

One day she's cold, she says It's complicated, she repeats her mantra about how it's *mixed*, the next she's saying Come here, pulling my chair up next to hers, laughing.

This morning I thought about Albert and the way she used to look at me sometimes, without saying anything, a long look she would hold for seconds at a time without smiling, without saying a word, not a harsh look, it was a look I never quite understood, one that wasn't meant for me. I almost called her. It seemed absurd, the fact that we'd split up. Then it didn't seem important at all. There's no such thing as heartache.

We get a drink in a chic-ish hotel, the vulgarity of chic and the charm of vulgarity. She's impressed by everything, even the photos of actors above the bar.

I love her less and that's exactly how she's always wanted me to love her. She thinks there's something beautiful about that. She doesn't understand that I'm faithful, that there are times when I've wanted to slap her.

4

I don't see my son anymore. Laurent says he's going to take care of him now to protect him. He says I'm not right in the head. He says I need help. He says I'm dangerous. He hints at things, pedophilia, violence, I don't know, he never finishes his sentences. He says he's paying people to show him all the things I like and post on Facebook. I wonder whether he also has someone following me or rifling through my trash. I look through the trash. Cigarette butts, chips, coffee, and empty boxes of veggie patties, which, granted, I don't eat like a normal person because I eat them cold with ketchup but at the end of the day does anyone really give a fuck? I went to see him to try and talk it out. There was food on the floor, moldy cereal under my son's bed, ashtrays everywhere. I wondered what the hell was going through his head. I wondered if it had anything to do with the fact that I brought up divorce the weekend before. Or the fact that Albert posted a picture on Facebook of me in a tuxedo and her sitting topless on my lap. He says he's collecting evidence. I could easily send him some of the pictures I have on my phone if he's that interested. Meanwhile, I've noticed that my son is being distinctly hostile toward me. Something quite violent about him. Maybe he's decided to hate me to make his dad happy. Maybe there's something else. I went to see the child psychologist. A skinny little blond, somewhere in the middle of the sixteenth arrondissement. She asked me if I loved my son. I looked at her red Lancel bag and her Hermès watch with the double strap and told myself it wasn't even worth answering. There's no way we have the same definition of love, she and I, and no, we probably don't talk to children in the same way either. I wondered how Laurent ended up choosing her. If he put out a call for bids to find the lousiest woman out there. I also wondered why he called her by her first name. I thought about my son, the little mensch. It's a Yiddish word, *mensch*, a word Robert taught me. A man, or a little man, with all the intelligence that it implies, someone who isn't fazed by anything. I decided I had to let him protect his father. He and I are strong. He and I both know about love. And I love him for his anger.

5

It's some kind of symposium, a vacation home with a mid-season atmosphere. It's all expenses paid and she's sneaking me in. I'm an added extra, the complimentary half bottle of sparkling wine at the hotel. Agnès is all over the place, worrying about everything. She doesn't want the slightest thing to imply that we're on this trip as lovers. She keeps repeating it, Not like lovers, it's become her obsession. She's barricading herself behind the words. And yet that's exactly what it is, a trip with a lover, wary and stingy. But even this half-assed desire is too much for her. I watch her worrying, hesitating, reeling, panicking. I leave her to it. I don't even know whether she's noticed that I don't talk much anymore.

Today she's decided we can stay a day or two longer, because the weather's going to be nice, she says.

It would be so easy to kiss each other, to lie down instead of worrying about going for dinner or how ugly the hotel is or what the weather will be like tomorrow, it would be so easy to not care about anything. She told me she likes to keep things casual, but deep down I don't think she's capable of that. Maybe I'm not either.

She seems to have gotten the gist that things were very sexual with Albert. She's decided she would like to try things after all. She gets up in front of me, she walks around, she leans out the window, she lingers there, she's wearing nothing but a cashmere sweater, she doesn't have any underwear on. What does she want, exactly? My tongue in her ass? Does she want me to clamp her nipples? I make a comment about the sky.

We're counting time, she and I. She touches my shoulder muscles, she says my body feels harder, she's worried about my tattoos. I look for the beauty I saw in her before, but all I can see is her falling apart, something beneath the skin making her body swell like a corpse.

At the hotel, she makes her bed, she says she feels uncomfortable leaving it for someone else to do. That's the kind of thing that's driving a wedge between our bodies each day.

She meets me after dinner, she left here early and got back late. I'm reading when she arrives. She's talking a little loudly, she's acting a little awkward. Maybe she's had too much to drink. She says I am going to bed and you are not going to touch me. She makes her declaration without me moving an inch, without me saying a word. The next day she's in a terrible mood for hours on end then suddenly she lies down next to me and says Kiss me. This brusque manner of hers, saying yes or no, but I'm not asking anything of her and she never seems to wonder if I am. Hasn't she learned anything about desire, the terrifying desire of the other, the desire that always says I don't know?

Beneath her perfume, I've always liked the faint smell of her sweat. Now I wrinkle my nose in disgust. It turns out she's just dirty.

Yesterday she made me come for the first time but it's not important.

6

I saw Albert again one evening. She was the one who called me. She was the one who invited me over. Candles everywhere, a special playlist, high black socks that almost look like stockings, black panties that accentuate her ass, white T-shirt, no bra, maybe a little makeup, the smell of cream, or it might have been oil. She staged an entire production. It was supposed to be a turn-on, which is precisely why it didn't work. She came or maybe she was just pretending. It was bad for me, too. I didn't stay over. We didn't call each other again.

7

There's always a moment when you see their face, the face of a drowning person, the expression they'll have when the time comes to die, all that despair. I watch Agnès struggling, fading, I watch her sink.

She says she never breaks up with anyone. But what about them? I wonder.

She's suddenly full of lofty words about some notes she asked me to write her a while back, though she barely acknowledged them at the time. I reread the slightly pompous emails I sent her, her replies, affectatious but curt, I delete the lot.

Suddenly it's all her crassness I see. It's always the same in the end, the body makes way for the weighing of souls.

A department store, clothes, fake chic, corpses milling around. Suddenly I see the extent of her desire, what she wants is things, all of her suffering is right there among the bric-a-brac that she can't have, that she's fascinated by. She wants to go shopping, buy herself bags, buy herself shoes. That's all she ever was, a provincial little woman.

She says that *freedom* is not enough, we need another word. Like a believer at the eleventh hour, like those who have never prayed, she proposes faith.

I lean toward the screen, over her shoulder, over her perfume, my face brushes against hers. I'm still protecting her, from her tiredness, her fear, the half life she's leading, my assassin's hands, I stop midgesture.

I could close my eyes, carry on smiling, remain in this limbo of politeness and cowardice, the only languages she knows. But I want it all to exist, falling in love and falling out of it too, whenever that happens. Otherwise, what's the point? What's the difference between good and bad?

8

Leaving her was easy. I ordered a Coke, she asked for a Perrier, I said I wasn't going to see her anymore. She smiled, she shook her head as if she didn't understand. I went to repeat myself. She stopped me midsentence because she never did want to talk about this thing between us, the thing she refused to name, the thing that involved her occasionally ending up with my head between her legs. She said No, you have to be kidding me. She said it again, shaking her head. Her bangs were shaking as well. I didn't say anything. She got up and left. I watched her walk away. Her quick, jerky steps. I told myself that her death wouldn't make the slightest difference to the global balance of energies. I told myself that the best part is always when it ends. When you find yourself alone again. When you've managed to get rid of the body. I wondered whether I was strange to think that way or whether everyone else was the same. I went to a place in Beaubourg that's open every day of the week including Sundays and holidays. I filled out a form, the guy disinfected my ear, he pierced it with a needle and slipped a titanium hoop through the hole.

9

It's such a stupid thing, money. Just ask poor people. They'll tell you how stupid it is. They know that when you don't work, you don't have any. Only the middle class think that when your family name's on Wikipedia you must automatically have money invested in mutual funds. Or a family behind you, giving you a hand. Families aren't like that, it reassures them to see one of their own fall, it makes them stronger, it's what they feed off. I know it was stupid to quit my job. I know I should have carried on working like before. I know it was always going to come back and bite me in the ass. I know I got what was coming to me for dicking around. The problem is I've never been able to take any of that seriously. I'm not a sensible person. Especially when interesting things are happening to me. It's such a rare occurrence. Still, I have to say, the timing was impeccable, not seeing my son meant one less mouth to feed. The gods had it all planned out.

10

Arrivals, 15:17, platform 2. I see them coming. I take off my headphones. My father is walking exceptionally slowly. Fanny looks even smaller than usual. She rarely comes to Paris. She's a little afraid. Before coming she said Isn't Montparnasse a bit complicated? I said Not really, but don't worry I'll be there. She packed his bag for him. For three days she's been talking about washing and ironing his pajamas. She's the one carrying the bag. I take it. It weighs a ton. I wonder what the hell she's put in there. He's clutching his bag of meds. An old military bag he brought back from Vietnam forty years ago. Very classy. I'll have to get that from him. Advance inheritance. It doesn't look like he's letting go of it any time soon, though. Just in case the pharmacy at the psychiatric hospital isn't good enough. Subutex, benzodiazepines, Xanax, and some other stuff I've never heard of. He even has vitamins in there. They're just as important as the rest according to Fanny. They both look tired. She tells me a woman on the train asked if my father was her husband. She told the woman she'd have killed him a long time ago if that were the case. She's been letting loose more lately. She says my uncles are assholes, my sister's a bitch, and my dad's a pain in the ass. I get it. He has that effect on everyone. I barely recognize his face, it's so white and puffy. That blank face, no longer expressive. He really is walking slowly. He might just be laying it on thick. It takes hours to cover the fifty meters to the taxi stand. He says Sorry I'm holding you up. As if I have somewhere to be. Fake politeness. Fake modesty. I talk about politics in the taxi. With the driver. When we get to Sainte-Anne, I ask for a wheelchair at reception. We look for the wing he'll be staying in. We look for the doctors. I leave my father in his room and go downstairs to sign him in. A young guy bums a cigarette from me. He asks me why I'm there, whether it's serious. I say I'm not the one staying here. I explain. I'm one of the normal people here. Like in court. Like in prison. He's the one who starts the conversation. I know I have to distance myself right away. That's what I do. I go back to see my father. He's with the intern. Not a bad-looking girl. I like the white coat. I guess my lawyer's robe must have the same effect. I wonder whether that's reason enough to stay in the job. He takes off his shoes. He has a hole in his sock. That upsets Fanny. I wonder what the hell she's doing here, for that matter, stuck in the middle of all this, with us. How she came to be his caregiver, how she never abandoned him, how she came to love him, really. I think about what an odd little team we make. The dyke, the ex-junkie, and the little old lady. But I guess it's normal for Sainte-Anne. Everything is.

11

I saw Albert's ex again. He told me he left the day he wanted to hit her. I tell him I often thought about him when she started spiraling on me, when she started going crazy. He stayed with her for a long time. He says he really tried to hold on. It wasn't even desire keeping him there anymore. He says he was never sure if she really came with him. We talked about her breasts, her ass, her skin. And that strange look of hers. The way she stares at you when she's fucking you. I told him about the last time I slept with her. He seemed happy to hear it wasn't all because of him. I thought to myself We both know exactly what it's like to love this girl, and if we were wondering if she ever acted differently, because I'm a woman and he's a man, now we knew she wasn't. I told myself it was OK to love a girl who's a bit lost, that's what we both wanted, he and I, a girl who has a gift for loving, a girl to fall in love with fast and hard and then fall out of love with and not have any regrets.

12

The psychiatric hospital is like a spa retreat for him, it always gives him a new lease on life. I go to see him twice a week. He sits in his armchair, I sit on the bed, propped up on one elbow, I take a newspaper, I flick through the pages. Every now and then we say a few words without looking at each other or else we just sit in silence. I don't tell him about my problems with Laurent and my son, or that I'm going to lose my apartment, I don't tell him I'm basically no longer a lawyer seeing as I never go to the office or to court or to the prisons, I don't tell him that I don't really have a solution for anything, I don't tell him about all the unexpected consequences, or that it's the unexpected I'm still looking for. I don't tell him there's no need to worry. That I'm always alright in the end. Am I always alright in the end? I flick through the pages of GEO. My sister brought it for him yesterday. I look at the absurd photos of tribes of men standing there naked. I wonder whether they really exist or whether they just answered a casting call for a photo shoot for readers who are so bored they're looking for escapism through something as stupid as a picture of some huts in a village with a bunch of guys living like it's the first day of creation. *GEO* makes me sick and *GEO* readers make me sick. Will I be alright in the end? A doctor arrives. Hello Doctor, would you like me to leave you to it? Yes, he would. I close the magazine. I put my jacket on. I leave.

13

We traveled second-class the day we went to open our bank accounts in Switzerland. We didn't buy tickets because we didn't have any money. We were probably both wearing jeans. I've never seen my father in anything but jeans, a tie, and loafers. Even when he was wasted. My grandmother the aristocrat had just died. She left some money for me and my sister. Not a lot, but something. She blew her entire fortune on I don't know what. Some ill-advised business venture, no doubt. And prime cuts of meat for her dachshund farm. She was six feet tall, she drove her Peugeot at full throttle with a Pall Mall hanging out of her mouth, and she bred dachshunds. Dachshunds were a ridiculous choice of dog for such a tall woman. I liked going to see her. She settled in Landes, she had a sheepfold on her brother's land, next to his château. A sheepfold in the middle of a pine grove with her dogs. And two foxes. She was a huge snob and she didn't give a shit about anyone. That suited me.

My mother was already dead when my grandmother died so the money went straight to us. We signed the paperwork, came up with stupid code names, and took something like ten thousand francs in bills folded up in our pockets. Big five-hundred-franc bills that made us feel like we were rich. At the station in Geneva, while we were waiting for the train, my father bought me a Bob Dylan CD and *Tommy* by the Who. That's what I put on when I go to Touraine. We don't talk, I just get out his old LPs with the Raoul Vidal record shop sticker still on the front and I put them on the turntable. Only one of the speakers works and it crackles but it's beautiful, the record the sleeve and even the sound. He's not in good enough spirits for *Tommy* anymore so I often put on "Girl from the North Country" with Johnny Cash. It's a song we both like. I watch him listening to it. Sometimes he sings. *For she was once a true love of mine.* I freaked out a bit when I went through customs but he was used to doing that kind of thing. He even used to make trips to Laos just to buy opium, which he sent to himself in Paris, general delivery, hidden in film spools. I didn't see much of that money and neither did my sister. My father emptied our bank accounts with the crappy code names for his drugs. And why not? We came back to Paris in first class. We paid for our return tickets. It's a good memory.

14

You get tired of everything eventually. Everything, my dear. Even people's misery. Even yourself. I got a phone call from some guy. His brother had killed an old woman. Then another one called. A guy who beat the shit out of his wife. When you're a scumbag talking to other scumbags, you can cut the bullshit. I was able to let go of my bourgeois preoccupations. Shake down the poor to make them cough up their cash. Either way their lives are fucked. I needed to keep hold of my Rolex. There's a considerable amount of bullshit I don't have time for anymore.

15

I went past the Flore the other day. There was a time when I used to go there a lot, in fact it's where I met Laurent, when we were both twenty. It was a Sunday, I went downstairs as I was, in jeans and a T-shirt I'd thrown on after swimming, my big arms and tattoos on show. People were staring. Especially women. I could tell I seemed odd to them. That's when I realized I had changed. I hadn't really thought about it before. It all happened gradually, without me noticing. An accumulation of tiny changes, the short hair, the tattoos, a collection of minuscule details that ended up changing the way I walk, the way I talk, maybe even the way I think. I realized I wasn't interested in the same books anymore, I didn't understand why Proust and all the others had been so important to me, my neighborhood felt too rich, too clean, too pretty, and even if I'd always worn jeans and T-shirts, maybe I was wearing them differently now, I didn't know how to dress for anything chic anymore, the old codes no longer came naturally to me. I thought about my son. I wondered whether he thought I was weird too. Whether that's why he was angry. I didn't have a clue. I was tired.

16

If you don't want to feel guilty, all you have to do is keep going. You can't get in the pool without taking a shower. So what I usually do is walk through the shower room quickly, without looking at anyone. But when I saw the woman standing there, I had to stop. A little lady in her sixties, slightly trashy. You can always tell, even when people are in swimsuits. It was her tattoos that struck me. I'd never seen anything like it. I'd never seen anything so beautiful. These weren't the kind of designs you go to Tin-Tin King of Tattoos or the big London studios for. This was more like hand stitching. She had the name Jean-Michel written all over her body, every which way. Jean-Michel I love you, Jean-Michel I want you, Jean-Michel I'm yours forever. She told me she'd had them for twenty years, and yes, she was still with Jean-Michel and yes, she was still fucking crazy about him. The best of all was the one on her back. In letters two inches tall across the left shoulder blade. Give me all your sperm. Anyone who doesn't find that more sublime than Hölderlin can go on their way. I wondered what there was left to write after a sentence like that. I wondered what you would write for a girl. I started thinking about love again.

17

Go fuck yourself.
Go fuck yourself.
Go fuck yourself.
Go fuck yourself.
Go fuck yourself.
Go fuck yourself.
Go fuck yourself.
Go fuck yourself.
Go fuck yourself.
Go fuck yourself.
Go fuck yourself.
Go fuck yourself.
Go fuck yourself.
Go fuck yourself.
Go fuck yourself.
Go fuck yourself.
Go fuck yourself.
Go fuck yourself.

Go fuck yourself.
Go fuck yourself.
Go fuck yourself.
Go fuck yourself.
Go fuck yourself.
Go fuck yourself.
Go fuck yourself.
Go fuck yourself.
Go fuck yourself.
Go fuck yourself.
Go fuck yourself.
Go fuck yourself.
Go fuck yourself.
Go fuck yourself.
Go fuck yourself.
Go fuck yourself.
Go fuck yourself.
Go fuck yourself.
Go fuck yourself.
Go fuck yourself.
Go fuck yourself.
Go fuck yourself.
Go fuck yourself.
Go fuck yourself.

I had one of those nights. Thinking about Laurent. I hired
a lawyer the next day. For the divorce and for my son. I
forgot to go swimming. You'll see, it'll be all right, things

will be just the same as before, it'll just be the two of us, but it'll be just like before. Bullshit. Everything has changed. I know I've brought chaos into his life with the chaos in mine. I know the whole thing must piss him off at times. We're all fucking selfish, parents, kids, he, I, it's no big deal, that's life, it'll all be fine. I know we love each other and we never lie. And anyway, for fuck's sake, the last time I saw him he told me he also wanted an earring in his right ear when he grew up and he said I could get a dragon tattoo on my back or maybe an eagle or another cool thing like that. It's not like he can have those kinds of conversations with his dad.

18

My father doesn't give a fuck about me being a lesbian anymore. Or maybe I'm the one who doesn't give a fuck so he's decided he doesn't either. All you have to do is say That's the way it is and everyone just deals with it. He also largely agrees that Laurent can go and fuck himself. So does my sister. We even have big lunches together on Wednesdays. Everything's great. We're getting on famously. Say, why don't we get a place where we can all live together? A little detached house on the outskirts of Paris? I went to see him in Saint-Mandé, the clinic where he's doing his aftercare therapy. It's crazy how close it is to Paris, Saint-Mandé. So I went on my scooter. We sat outside. We drank coffee and smoked cigarettes. I figured that at this point, I might as well tell him I smoke. He talked about drugs. He talked about opium, the first time in Cambodia, how the opium was never a problem, how it was the heroin that changed everything. He told me it was in his genes, he was sniffing ether at the age of fourteen.

He said I had it in my genes too, but he was talking about girls. He told me there was a phrase he'd learned to say in twenty languages, Japanese, Italian, Malay, Khmer, Chinese, German: Hello madam, that's a beautiful dress. He told me he felt as though he'd lived several lives. Each of them as intense as the last. Traveling, drugs, and love. He asked me what stories I could tell about my mother. I said I didn't know.

19

What is a dead person? Nothing. A pile of bones somewhere. Something nobody remembers. You can tell
whatever story you want. You can take all those little
bones, put them in any order you like, recreate a skin, put
it in clothes, make a puppet, stand it up, make it walk and
kiss and yell, give it intentions, a meaning, invent dia-
logues and conversations. You can make up anything. You
can imagine whatever life you want for the dead. But I
don't believe in all that. The dead are not important to
me. There's nothing between them and us. No sadness. I
don't know who my mother was and I don't need to
know. I could tell stories about her life, or what I knew of
it. I could tell the story of her childhood in the Basque
country with the Irish nanny, her father the politician,
minister of state under Pétain, but also member of the
Resistance, sent to Fresnes by the Germans then deported
to Plansee, the father who was sent to trial at the High
Court after liberation, the father who fell from grace. I

could tell stories about the dogs, the hunting, the countryside, the horses, stories of a world that lived in stories, in the books we read in the châteaux, all that romanticism, and how it ends up warping our understanding of life and what we expect from it, I could tell the story of a class of society in sudden decline, a generation that grew up with twenty servants and ended up cleaning up after themselves in housing projects, a generation that hates the class it came from and never managed to find its place, I could tell the story of a family of four sisters, suicidal or crazy, junkies or alcoholics, four tall, dark, and beautiful sisters who spent their childhoods in their navy-blue uniforms with the nuns at the boarding school, I could tell the story of the upper class of the sixties, the freedom and affluence, the apartment on rue Bonaparte in the building designed by the imperial baron, I could tell the stories of all the parties and all the deaths. I could tell the story of how my parents met at the age of twenty, how they loved each other and left each other a dozen times over, a story that belongs only to them, one I only observed from afar. I could tell the story of the childhood I spent clinging to her legs, glued to her at all times, her olive skin, her perfume. I could tell endless stories about her. Her driving her car, always taking us to restaurants, the after-school snacks at the café, the nursery rhymes she would sing to me, the scrambled eggs at the Tea Caddy, lunches at Le Canton, dinners at the Vieux Casque, the hours she'd spend putting on makeup in front of the mirror, the serious tone she had when talking to children, the puppies she delivered, my mother the sorceress, her taste for words, almost physical, her taste for all things. I could tell the story of the time just before her death, when I'd overtaken her in height and how strange it felt, to be just a little taller than her, or her bangles jangling about her wrists on those evenings in the countryside while I was falling asleep, the way she moved her feet, her wide mouth, her narrow hips, the foreign look about her that made everyone ask where she came from, I don't know where she got it, her Basque blood, I suppose. I could talk about her obsession with beauty, her own primarily, but the beauty of others, too. That animal quality she had, that tension, that desire, that constant friction between boredom and joyfulness, something you might call intensity. But did I see it right? Was it actually like that? And what does it matter? The dead are quiet and gentle. The dead are nothing.

20

It's funny, I never thought of my father as Jewish. But the great thing about Robert is that he suggests words to provide an alternative explanation as to why things are going so badly. For him, the height of stupidity is people asking how you are. How are you? How are you doing? How can you possibly give an intelligent answer to a question like that? Robert takes depression very seriously, he sees it as something you have to make the absolute most of. He was there this morning, at the Palette, with his floral shirt and that old tattoo on his arm, telling me how good his hypnotist on rue des Mathurins has been, for everything, including Léna, and that's when he said that my father was the most Jewish of all Jews, with all that guilt, with all the guilt of the Jewish people put together, and that if he were to walk by, right here, right this minute, he wouldn't be able to say anything to him, because he knows that behind the tie and all the courtesy, my father's guilt, which stems from his Jewishness, his fundamental, structural essence, prevents him from uttering a single word, to the point where he's no longer even able to breathe. For Robert, when you're a Jew you're a Jew, and the odd Catholic marriage in your family tree doesn't make a blind bit of difference. When you're smart, life is tough, and when life is tough, you're a Jew. Not necessarily in that order. I thought to myself *Junkie, Jew,* or *dyke,* it's all the same, they're just different words for the same thing. When you're like Robert or my father or me, you just have to choose one of the three and stick with it, the reality it represents is irrelevant. Deep down, being gay means nothing to me, just like being Jewish means nothing to Robert, just like being a junkie means nothing to my father. There's no substance to any of it. Nothing of importance. Nothing essential. Robert, my father, me, Albert, even Laurent, though he doesn't realize it, we're all doing really badly. That's how it is, that's how we were born. So we're forced to try things to try and get better. Being Jewish or gay or a junkie, for example. Sometimes it works for a while. Sometimes it doesn't. Either way you have to do something with the longing, the absence. So what about you, why are you gay? My friend Jibé and I decided that would be a good question to ask. No more than one sentence, please. Answers on the back of a postcard. You can swap *gay* for *Jew* or *junkie* or whatever you want. Or just *unhappy*, without giving it a label.

21

The weather's nice, vacation is over, I'm on my way home from school. I run into my father downstairs. We live in social housing near Montparnasse, we got in by pulling some strings. He tells me to go to my grandparents' house, my mother has collapsed, she's in the hospital. My parents have no money now. No money for an apartment, no money for heroin. They drink cheap whiskey they buy from the convenience store nearby run by the Chinese family. He locks himself in his room and drinks there alone. No more jetting around the world to report on major events, no more having shirts made specially in Bangkok. My sister and I are always with my mother. She's six, my sister, then seven then eight. We're always on the lookout for signs my mother has been drinking. We examine her eyes, the way she smells, the way she speaks. She starts talking nonsense, battling with her pride, her brilliance has been drowned in alcoholic squalor. I yell at her. I hate doing it, it's horrible to speak to her like that, but I can't help it. I even got into a physical fight with her once. My uncle the doctor wants to talk to me. We go into my grandfather's office. He uses technical and precise language, *cerebral hemorrhage*. He asks whether I agree they should switch off the machines. It feels like a rhetorical question, I say yes. He asks if I want to see her in the hospital, I say no. I don't cry. I go back into the living room. They haven't told my sister yet. My father is pouring himself whiskey after whiskey. The crystal decanter is on a sideboard under a portrait of a marshal of the empire. The sideboard is made of black marble. My grandmother is smoking. She tells my father not to drink too much, it won't do any good. He shrugs his shoulders.

22

We started following each other on Instagram. I asked her out for coffee. She agreed to go for a beer. I ended up taking her for dinner. At some point she stopped talking, looked at me, and smiled. I walked her back to her motorbike. I didn't want to take her back to my place. I hadn't cleaned up so I wouldn't feel obliged. I said I'm still going to kiss you though and I kissed her before she put her helmet on. The moment I held her and felt her ribs and breasts against me was the moment I thought that I might want her. The next day I sent her a text asking her over for lunch the following day. She said OK, she came over, we spent the afternoon in bed. And so it went on. It didn't take long for me to love her. First her body. Then the rest of her. The week after that I didn't love her anymore. I ended it via text. It's never pretty anyway so who cares how you do it. We met up one last time, she gave me back my T-shirt and I gave her back the book she lent me that I never read. Maybe I felt guilty, maybe

I just wanted to see how far I could go, maybe it was because the weather was nice that day, but in any case, I slept with her again. I don't know whether it was a good idea. It's going OK but I'm getting a little bored. The problem is that even with girls, it's all become banal. It's just sex, just love. Nothing new. Nothing life-changing.

ABOUT THE AUTHOR

Constance Debré left her career as a lawyer to become a writer. She is the author of a trilogy of novels: *Playboy* (Prix de La Coupole, 2018), *Love Me Tender* (Prix *Les Inrockuptibles*, 2020), and *Name*.